© 2025
Sam Moe
I Might Trust You

Published by: Experiments in Fiction
Cover Art by: Sam Moe
Cover Design by: Experiments in Fiction

ISBN-13: 978-1-7394044-9-9

I MIGHT TRUST YOU

Experimental Short Fictions

SAM MOE

Praise for *I Might Trust You*

"Sam Moe's *I Might Trust You* invites readers to luxuriate in the delicious language of heartache. A master imagist, Moe allows us to step inside each experience of discovery—be that of self, lover, or other—and to linger alone with the taste of each sensual experience. Honest, vivid, passionate, these short stories will leave you simultaneously breathless with excitement and decimated by grief. Moe serves up an intimate, vulnerable array of complex emotion and delivers an incisive look at the painful truths that make each of us human."
—Alicia Shupe, author of *Beneath an Indiana Tree*

"*I Might Trust You* showcases Sam Moe's endlessly inventive voice. Her prose glitters, and her images—vividly painting sunflowers, seances, false moons, fillet knives, cat collars, cut candles, and so much more—gleam. In these pages, we encounter the many shapes of loss, loneliness, longing, and love. Throughout, we feel as if we are in the presence of a storyteller who knows the secrets of our beautiful and broken world. This is a fantastic collection."
—Bradley Sides, author of *Crocodile Tears Didn't Cause the Flood*

"Sam Moe's *I Might Trust You* is an act of literary alchemy—unraveling like a fever dream, where memory slips into myth and language pulses with intimacy, longing, and the quiet ache of transformation. This is a book that does not merely tell a story; it moves like an incantation, revealing love and loss in fragments that shimmer at the edges of consciousness, both wound and salve at once.

Moe's writing is hypnotic and immersive, evoking through sensory detail the warmth of a kitchen where devotion is folded into food; the sea thrumming with promises; the ghost of a lover dissolving into myth. Each piece feels like something remembered and half-forgotten, something whispered in the dark.

Lyrical, haunting, and breathtaking in its depth, *I Might Trust You* is a book that doesn't simply invite you in—it enchants you.

Moe's work reads prismatic and renders you dizzy in its inventiveness. Moe might leave you speechless."

—C. Heyne, author of *My Room (and Other Wombs)*

Acknowledgements

Thank you so much, Ingrid, for accepting this collection, and to all the lit mags who have published versions of these stories and supported my writing journey. This collection would not be possible without the love and support of my found family, Daniela Cornelius, David St. John, Beth Boswell, Dave Boswell, Eric Smith, Ryan Brown, Joseph Robertshaw, and Alanna Frost. *Esto es atemporal.* Thank you for saving my life when I was drowning. *Más allá de donde el diablo perdió su poncho, confío en ti.*

Contents

1. Dinner

Cherry

Farmhouse days and I am unraveling like veins. There's nothing to tell. Patches of grass and amber kitchen lights, soft hallways and your mother's plants, your loyalty is messy, you have an affinity for eighteen types of strawberries; your middle name tells a story. Promise I don't care too much about you, promise my journal is filled with everyone's name but yours, this isn't a surrender or a lie, this is a sweetheart jam and compound butter with bits of spinach and melted duck fat, this is my favorite time of day, when you've been tricked into spending time near me, but enough is enough, what I really want is to know whether you believe me about the blood. Everywhere, people we know at the dinner table, high heat and flushed cheeks, wine glasses dotted with rhinestones, silverware stamped with words like *fever* and *sailor*, I don't know how to convert my love into a book, these days what am I trying to say. And when the old floor—imported from a barn where once, many cats, your crush pressed into a pillar, straw in your hair, I was but an owl observing, I gave my heart away to a field mouse and who knows what happened to the organ, dear god, I wanted to be the candle flame and the space between your thumb and forefinger—sinks in on itself, and the party guests fall into the earth, this soft green cave of ivy and grief and even bats, when that happens, reach for me. I need to go it alone but still, save my life. Alone come dusk. Wish you would hold me in the kitchen but there are more important things to do, like stare at the navy sky, porch licked clean from rain, shiny frogs are red gemstones from mother's brooch, it matters too much, the roosters are all laying blue eggs, I got my blood in the forest and then some, want you to say what you would have done if you were there. The options: put a stop to things / feed me to the bears / turn me into a dog / turn yourself into a dog / bear witness / celebrate the months without bandages / do I still matter / clean the drain of clots / my ribcage will truly destroy things between us. And honestly, if this were the last thing I could say—the scream at dawn, the heavy knock while your left hand is holding three dishes cooked by your new love, she has such soft brown hair, if there is no more dancing and Saturdays seep into the sink hole, and earlier that day you kissed her face then forgot my name, maybe then we could talk about tucking complication into bed, leaving town for slow mud walks and she's exiled from dinner—I'm a regret; the kitchen is so warm and inviting I forget myself.

Mother

Drunk at the table, eating from a plate of oysters, each gold-lipped, a mixture of melted butter the color of sun, heroic Rockefellers hard to eat, being fed to you by him one hand under the table on your thigh, the other at your mouth, dinner is an experience. I am wearing my wish earrings, meaning, hope you're enjoying my show, hope you still love me when we get home, just two Geminis, daughters of horse owners, women who pray to gods, women who wear tops made of flowers, I don't want to kill myself anymore, you don't care, there is a phone in the center of the table, grey as concrete, small knife scars in the plastic, the man who might be called a father or a husband is waving, swatting at the chandelier, twisting light, halo casts, across the room no one cares, now they're all saints, my sister at the window behind our table admiring herself, pony-printed dress, flower in her hair, from another father, heart a carousel of opportunities, bright spaces, zebras for love, whales for singing, open-faced petunia for restoration, I can no longer name what happens inside a body, I am ghostly at the fine dining table, I am not you, I've learned, don't budge, don't find myself in the company of glue, maybe I'm lying, maybe I'm water / leaving / daughter / son / cherry tomato /

addicted / easy to leave / bad / at learning / my lessons.

Later; guests whisper into after-dinner coffee, candles worn down to red lumps, I excuse myself from the table, to the bathroom where women with haloed crowns wait, they tuck me into a soft napkin basket, I am newly used linens, I am a person / mother and other / daughter and other / daughter still, meaning third daughter from the table near the doorway, come stand at the mirror, do each other's hair, ignore the women, saints, wearing glow-in-the-dark necklaces, they are ready to leave, they will eat father. I'm August and the suffocating wave during back-to-back king tides, I've eaten all the pearls from the sea, it's late and when I'm finally back home, yes, if you're wondering, death still looms, hate still crawls through hands and mouth, I fall for an addict, he ruins my life, he ruins my friends he reminds me of a father, he sells and uses what little money he has left to buy me chilled bottles, sea-foam green, iced teas, new shoes, says it's not like me to be a daughter instead of dinner.

Feast Day

Chilly grey air, rain for days, a deep desire to pluck the buttons off his coat and swallow them whole. You tell someone you're writing but not about who. Still, the cheese board separating you from your crush, pearl apples, glittering blue-green grapes, slow-growth ham with pale pink lightning bolts of flavor, *bresaola*, desire, robust cheese and amber wine, your heart walks around on stilts, fresh herbs then edible flowers, you wish someone would bind your hand to the drawer. Wrong, the way night falls like steam then navy as the waves which dragged you and your grandmother under, you knocked your knees into rocks and fish, she laughed hysterically, what is this feeling in the face of such loss. Overall, the evening is luxurious. Your pants are so soft they could be pajamas. He tells jokes about a daughter you never knew existed, his kitchen is coated in wheat-stamped tiles, a black tie loose around his neck, stop staring at yourself in the mirror, stop trying to catch his words in your palm. Don't you feel conflicted about the Humboldt fog, how you want to wear the cheddar cloths around your shoulders like a cloak, dig yourself a shallow grave in the cellar, you are jester and meadow and broken at the wrists. You are blue cheese, sticky oil, a raincoat wanting for shoulders. Why turn your feelings to *confit*, what about the internal cherries, perhaps slip into something a little sweeter, tongue on whipped cream coated butter knives, press goat cheese to hives, pretend France was so many summers ago, pretend you don't know the feeling of his mouth on your collarbone.

Red/Restaurant/Cherry/Father

There is pincushion moss and there is this dizzying red tomato that you slice into thirds, then eighths. I watch you arrange the small red pieces, like checkers, never hearts, until you have created a centerpiece so sweet it turns my cheeks hot. We are in the midst of service, taking care of the indoor plants so they don't grow out of control onto the guest's plates, wrapping rubber bands around our fingers so we don't feel the scald of the hot plates. Will you look after me, after all is said and done?

There are chandeliers with ribbons hanging around their centers, we are careful to avoid the lightbulbs so as not to burn beneath the glow. And I don't see the fathers anywhere, I think they have disappeared into the private dining suites so they can discuss wallpaper colors and biscuit consistency. The fathers do not care that I am at dinner, that we are engaging with each other.

You busy? You ask.
I shake my head no.
Do you want to be?

Of course I do, so I take the knife out of your hand

and begin to slowly cut into the honey bulbs. They ooze out sweetness, and their hard outer shells are orange as a sun.

It could be helpful if I stayed by your side for the rest of the evening. There is a Saturn loneliness, the kind that you can't store inside of coffee filters or seed bags. The kind of loneliness that turns into a ghost who slams the cabinet doors. This ghost needs a hug. This ghost does not like the color blue.

There are party guests with champagne flutes that look like toys, and someone tells you a rumor, but you only catch the tail-end. There is a bathtub in the center of the room with a small sign next to it that says *don't* and there are boughs of red clay made to look like dough, twisted into galettes, with ceramic blueberries nestled in the center.

I should like to abandon my heart, I tell you. You nod your head, focused on the task at hand. There are true pears to be sliced, never peeled, there are hurts, eyes carved into forks and knives, the restaurant is in full bloom. But I was never meant to return, yet here I am, again and again I hide my body in the space between the registers and the ice cream bar. The servers all know my name, but we are not friends, there is a thunderstorm going on outside, but I see no lightning, there is something beating in my chest that I don't have a name for, and there is you, taking my hand and tugging me down the hallway towards the cooler.

Where the best cherries are hidden, you say, fishing in the ice, like cold gems the size of fists, betwixt are cherries that remind me of my mother, cherries like the holidays all smelling of well-whiskey. Am I truly at home, with you, or do I just not feel scared when you take my head in your hands? I don't want to return to service. I know there are guests who are hot, guests who don't know how to tie bowties, guests who think they know my name, but they don't. And the lamps are ribbed like pineapples, and the restaurant sign flickers on and off, I am tying and retying my apron as you take the pits from my mouth.

Where are the fathers, you ask, and I shrug. *How should I know,* I reply. There are hundreds of fathers, thousands of fathers more, still waiting in the vestibule, for their eldest daughters to return to them. We are busy hiding, we are busy becoming twisted and exhausted beneath disco lights, we are no longer women, and we dislike the fathers.

I was going to return home, to an empty house, but everyone wants me to stay for conversation and criticism. The hours twist; it's late, there are empty beer bottles and a man leaning against the bar with a handful of old popcorn. Soon we will light candles and candies on fire, soon fathers will cheer as we hand them their dinners. I do not know where the others are, the sisters and the siblings and the parrots. There are no mothers, there is only us and this burning sensation I mistake for love. Rather than telling you how I feel, maybe I could tell you to press right here, into the space between my thumb and forefinger, until the scar disappears. I want soup and I want Band-Aids that don't hurt when I rip them off. I wish my hair weren't green, I wish I weren't the daughter who threw the confetti, the daughter who hates roses, the daughter with new scars and old scars, stomach aches, grapefruit perfume. I want to be around that summertime feeling, when June and July hold hands, and I forget I have a family.

I don't want to be an embarrassment, I don't want to eat cilantro, I don't want to fall in love with mozzarella cheese water and the way you laugh when you're cooking. I begin to forget we are in the kitchen; I forget which stove is the tricky one, which lobster claw is the poisonous one. I am not sorry, and I am not good at telling the truth.

Maybe we can leave together and lay on the embankment. There will be stars whose names we can't remember, and these stars will be hidden behind the clouds. Loud and blue-yellow enter the lightning bolts into the sky, but we aren't going to get burned, we aren't beautiful enough to be turned into gods.

Soon it is twelve, soon I am sorry I am not around as often as I would like, soon we walk out in a pack of twenty-five, each of us modeling the three-plate carry, some of us wearing bags slung over our shoulders that are filled with ice and wine, dripping a thin trail of cold like an irritated slug, but it doesn't matter because the fathers are impressed, the room is glorious, there is no imposter syndrome, there is no love, there is only a thin veil of separation between their plates of food and the knife which severs the meat.

Goldfield

You arrive at the party last, reckless as sunflower,
you don't want the others to know you traded lungs
and then some to get through the doors, everybody
knows that you're ridiculous, who else would look
good wearing that citrine dress, tourmalines in your
ears, you're into honey and her cooking, you love ex-
cess and you came with the appetite, you came with
the pen, the desire to cut throats, do you remember
staying up late in the Slumber Hall whisking eggs until your wrists hurt, your eyeliner was smudged but
you didn't care, told your ex you had forgotten something at the store and she mumbled someone else's
name in her sleep so you left for the hotel, the chefs
love when you sit on the counters, calling you *bold*
and *sunshine*, skin the lemons for the dish, skip the
tablecloths, take your no-bakes into the craft room,
accept that the drinks you are given aren't potions
for transportation, you can write yourself out of this
life, fondant fancies and bring the rum, darling don't
let lemon curd become more charming than you,
don't bring mother into this, she looked so pissed at
the pool, toying with water lilies while yelling at the
neighbor, you've left it all behind, magic and lime,
threw the marriage proposal in the trash, you pretend to be strong but you're tripping over your dress,

you're wishing you had fangs, praying to the old gods to sharpen the butter knives and the only saint who listens is a desperate man carving letters into the silverware, he stares at you from the dining room and asks why you even bother, let's show everyone what you can do with a limoncello, God knows you can make a tasty margarita, you cry at night in your room and your ex never mailed your things, lost socks with wolves and winter orange whiskey recipes, she's sipping a mango float somewhere and cursing you by both names, this isn't about truth or love, this isn't even about whether or not the kitchen is full of monsters, no, this is about how you paid your dues, swept dupe receipts and washed floors, now you're sweetened like fruit, they let you slice the fish with your fingers, they hand you ramekins of slushie, everything sparkles and the chandelier looks so brilliant you dream daily about eating it, you save your own life and you save the crumbs from the overtakes, your coworkers and fellow servers are calling you an angel, sweet as cake mix cookies, they don't know how you imitate art, screw the mimic and the woman at the clinic who told on you to your mother, and while you're at it, take, in no particular order: their hearts, pants, pears and satin handkerchiefs, a drink called smash, her high heels you loved so much, discarded matches and soy milk, those kisses that make your lips bleed, apple juice, and any knives you can get your hands on.

Once more into the nicotine

There are wolves at the wedding and fish in the bathtub. Earlier you took the fillet knife to my throat and told me if I ruined things, you would leave my body at the altar. *Your late mother's rug,* I corrected as you pressed the soft part of the metal until my breath hitched. Little do you know it's not about ruining things, like love or a perfectly good glass of vodka, neat. So you don't get things twisted, this isn't about the time you left me in the middle of the forest with the rocks and the soot and the webs and the crane. I carved your name into the base of every tree; you didn't care. It wasn't me who hot-wired your car or seduced your doctor, we didn't break up on the bus but at the bookstore downtown, everyone on the 1 train was asking why I was sobbing, men were giving me cards with their phone numbers inscribed in deep purple ink, a woman looked up from a book she was reading and rolled her eyes, the glitter belt I wore felt too tight and my mom texted to ask if I left the house again looking like the 90s. I didn't have the heart to tell her we'd ever met. You, drinking a beer in the middle of a convenience store and stoned again at the pizza plaza, you with cotton candy tattooed on your left wrist and a dimple in your chin, chain-smoking you, sucking on a red vine like it was a lollipop and not a piece of sweet red wax, you deserve to get your heart broken again, this isn't about the wedding reception, it's not even about the cigarettes. But here we are on the balcony of your parent's estate, me with my cheap suit and you with Juliet wings, *to complement my vibe or whatever* you say before flicking ash onto your grandfather's head. He'll never notice, he's too focused on buckets of silver sword philodendrons, the hofstras and the hybrid centuries, snapping a pocketknife open and closed like a jaw. Beyond is your soon-to-be wife, bottle of champagne in one hand, a petit filet mignon in the other, no one cares where she went to school, they're too busy gushing over her shoes, others still are rolling joints in the kitchen and singing. You've got this look in your eye like you don't want to have ever loved me, you wish you could cover up the tattoos, set the pictures on fire, unknit the yarn, maybe if you tried hard enough you could wish the salmon and sea urchins back to the shore, you could scream a lobster's joins together, you hate your voice is like glue, you owe me seventy-five dollars, you should think long and hard about the way sunlight filters through the trees in fall, you should stop playing with the lighter, you should forgive me but you won't. Instead, we head into the house. We eat someone else's chicken in a bucket. The music starts and someone is giving a speech, but you give me this look

like you don't mind forking over money for gas if I
drive the car, so I hot-wire the mustang while you cry
from laughing so hard.

That summer, my heart was an apple

Rope-homes for crabs, sand mixed with your bottle caps, domesticated lobster legs waving, the napkin your father used at dinner, its surface stamped with the town's name and someone's initials, those days I woke late to find the two of you in bed next to me, early nineties shows playing on a faded laptop, I have tracked salt into the house again, I am praying for the clouds to eat away at my heart until it's nothing more than a seed-studded core, could be sharpened into a paring knife, could be used to take his heart as my own. He walks the edge of water, waving at seals, unaware sharks pass nearby, he told me I wasn't easy to love and that's why he wasn't attracted to me anymore, he proposed to me in the liquor aisle of a supermarket and I lost the ring, my stone is opal, not topaz, everyone knows that, but what does it matter, we're about to drive through mist-sticky cream-seafoam bubble towns, we're going to get lost near inflatable beach toy vendors, we'll fight loudly at the motel, get kicked out, his daddy has money so we get to see a pool at night, lilac against the strange sky, I wish I could make this work, instead I leave almost as soon as we arrive, abandoning crustacean-crates-turned-bookshelves, there are noodles in drawers, I broke a blender, no one sees me and when I return,

New England parts its leaves for Autumn but I pretend it's for me, and I am officially a sand-licked ghost, I sleep in the ash room, I smoke on the porch, and loneliness twists like a screw into lungs.

Dicentra

Winter

I am in love with the sous-chef and her flower bundles she brought for a candy special, I watch as she coats peach and lilac in a thin cloak of sugar, she wears arrows in her ears, and I feel bad my arms are empty. I peel nail polish from my cuticles, I am as lost as I was months ago, when all this first began, my heart is always too affected by food, I have recurring dreams about organs coated in apple skins and necklaces of pear seeds, I wake starving, I can't remember if it's December or spring, I don't want to be alone.

Spring

I wonder if she would go with me, to the forest of yellow-green leaves, we could talk about their resemblance to butternut squash, we could be lit; I used to walk through sprinklers at night, I sat on guard rails and ran around the woods behind the house, I never knew my way around the sand, but I didn't have to, there was always someone near to hold the flashlight as we walked through the streets. I wish I could listen to bird songs while we cook, instead I am humming and helping with the honey jars, there is a breeze from the back door, the wood is chipping and it's just as well, this building is faded, smells vaguely of sunscreen and salt, we lay our bacon out to dry on the back porch, will she recognize me after time has passed?

Summer

June nights I have a dream I try to put mascara on. The brush accidentally touches my nose, and flowers begin to spill from my face. I doodle the word *bloom* on the insides of my fingers, I think about your heart for hours. Maybe my memories are meant to be doughy in the summertime, what month is it anyway? I'll lay out my feelings and flaky croissant-dough hearts one by one on the table until I figure out what is true and what is merely a result of the season. I still don't know what I'm trying to say to her.

Fall

It's late, an evening. When she asks for help I follow her into the walk-in freezer with a crate, standing quiet as she loads the box with begonias, clover, fuchsia, hollyhock, linden, roses, bundles of sugar cubes bound in cloth, a wine made of sunflowers, edible glitter, six ribeye steaks, a chilled butcher's knife with the words *hello, heaven* etched in the side, overripe cherries, salted cream, fudge, hummingbird cake, sesame oil, an oyster that someone has written on with sharpie—that says *love* that I think we both pretend not to see, and a bottle of horseradish, and

a vial of gold flakes, and a jar of tomato sauce, and
a glass orb whose ingredients need to be shaken up
into a braid.

Instructions for dinner

Springtime. The permanent swoop of a goose neck. Times you lay in tall grass, everything a mix of hazel and forest-green, everywhere you go, cover it. Savor the healing, give up on your love of marsh land and yellow swamp. You bring yourself home then walk yourself back from the ledge. Again. Don't speak of the past. Don't turn into a sullen copper mare at dinner. No one can stand your hooves, your partying, your allusions. You are underneath the table while the adults plan dinner, you are in trouble, there are no rules. Eat every single part of the pear, even the bones, even the little lime-skin house. Climb inside yourself again and again. Light matches. Say *sorry*. Say *these are troubling pasts, these are splits in skin*. Crying on the Red Line, smear your paint on an unsuspecting woman's coat. For one month you can only eat fries. When everyone toasts, pretend you're not sick. They bring you a trough of champagne and everyone laughs when you can't eat, tossing honey-glazed carrots into your drooling maw. Share hands with someone you shouldn't. Somehow, the lighting is all wrong. Your body is all wrong. The sick about the sickness is you bear the illness. Someone has drawn a creature on the chalkboard advertising beers named after candies. When anyone asks, leave your hands on the table. Unfortunately, the relapse ranges from scratch to wound. The doctor told you to take care. Certainly you were once a human girl, now you are a farm horse, don't run your course, you know what they always say. You're so hot beneath the lamps. When they feed you sugar cubes, accept they are not punishments. Take off your shirt in the bathroom and think about your blood vessels in the cold, pale light. Your hands look like small racehorses and your tongue, my god, is a crime scene. Shut up. Don't be bad when you are touched. Don't be scared by the presence and absence of love.

Recipe

It is my intention / to have you talk into my ear / not
quite over this / not quite love / forgive the risk / my
selfish little gaze / the smother and gauze of my heart
/ grape juice instead of wine / we pretend to be ready
/ for rebirth / can others see the hunger / this mis-
shapen haunt / I think *nunca más* and yet / thought
you'd bring cigarettes / thought you were as pretty
cómo una perla in an oyster's gum / *cómo mi* / *cómome*
/ *pero* / not falling yet / summer storm / chalice once
filled with jam / what a pretty peach you are / what's
in it for my heart is five percent of yours / your freezer gem shining like a jewel / you're bad at making
coffee / want mornings / I'm not sweet but I pretend
to be / but really truly, I'm sorry / to my core / about
the begging / strawberry basil / lemon-blueberry /
you don't have to say anything / I already know / you
wish for strawberry-kiwi / you wish for mothers / I
think I am your hunger / can we talk about space /
luscious blue and honey berry / it's been a long while
since I've had fresh lies / please be my goat / I am
your ram / let's work the mirror to death / my apri-
cot / my last slice of cake / let's fall asleep on the 1
train together / let's go downtown / don't look at me
like you know / but I know you know / about the
sequins and the seashells / I just love the sea you hide

in jars / keep my fake heart in the foyer / take my real
heart and slide it on toast / maybe one day we'll be
back on the farm / I'll be your knife / you'll use me
to slice bread / don't you want breakfast sauce / don't
you know how to turn impulses into violets / wear
me like a crown / I'm only out of control because of
the orange jelly / sticky fingers / buttermilk and marmalade / please / add a little more sugar to the water.

Say

It's okay dinner is shaped like a fish but made out
of honey and drizzles of cranberry, there are peels
of gouda, there are coconut strands, your mother's
kitchen is all steam, say the rain stops—and it will—
should we go for mussels and garlic toast or should
I spend all day pretending to write when I know as
well as you do I'll never be able to capture the Sauvignon Blanc, life is a yawn and then there's passion
fruit, I say I love gooseberry but really I mean wings
of honeydew, I mean clingstone and donut, some
days I feel like I'm arctic supreme with you, maybe
nectarines, say you know my mind has melted like
butter with rosemary, say I'm flavorful, say I'm okay,
I'm your perfect scallion slice, I am your long-sim-
mered chicken stock, just say I'm yours and we can
make jumbo crabcakes in the hot tub, say you choke
on linguini coated in crushed red pepper and cloves,
would you look to me for help or elsewhere, please
admit I am simmering, I am spring, I am so sweet
you wouldn't even mind the blood, let's say I tell you
about the blood anyway, the times I opened old journals and bandages fell out, I am a skip away from a
new scar, I haven't yet told you but I relapsed on the
beach and all the couples were eating lobster rolls on
butter buns, there were children sitting in the surf,

my friend tells me eventually I'll be brave enough
to say words like *suicide*, I'm anxiously switching
out blood for shells, every time I say potato I mean
I'm one step closer to telling you about burning, red
bowl, thick stock, okra so soft it could be cut with
a fork, I play with a paring knife beneath the table,
I dream about telling my mother what happened, I
dream about you, warm bread, tangy *pescado frito*,
say my grandmother's hands are here, just say it—
smoked trout, stone fruit, snapping peas, saffron and
cigarettes—but why can't you just say squid, shrimp,
scallion, summertime-style spice, sea, slow, starve.

Margherita Pizza

I guess what I'm trying to say is this. Christmas Eve and my stepsister is over. She hates me and I don't know why. I gift her a small ceramic champagne bottle in a white box. The bottle is a charm, and its neck is filled with gold and silver bells. She gives me nothing. I want to tell her not to worry, I can make myself even more unlovable. Instead, I walk around the street near my childhood home in a sweatshirt and pajama pants. I wish the weather would have mercy. Back inside, I eat four everything bagels with cream cheese and drink punch made with whiskey, bourbon, and three bottles of champagne. I don't normally drink. I don't know how to soften. I tell stories of when I was younger and dating two different heroin addicts. My mother finds this story funny, now. How she thought I was on drugs, too, until she found out I wasn't. No one asks how they fell into my life; no one knows I just needed protection. I didn't realize protection also takes. Protection pushes you into the back seat of a car and you disassociate while looking at the moon. Anyway, my mother tells stories of how she wrote a letter to G about rearranging his face if he ever came near me again. I always wondered where he went. We used to eat pizza slices in his dark green Cadillac. He laughed when I stole thongs from department stores. He brought me to different houses to kiss all his friends. He was forty and I was seventeen. C was no different. For years after I tried to move on he would call me from jail. To be clear, I didn't put him there. I rode the commuter rail to Boston and my body was covered in blood and no one asked if I was okay. I wish I had stories about salvation. I wish the women in my family loved me. I keep track of things they say at dinner, in a blue notebook that says *crack is wack*, a miniature photo of the Keith Haring mural. My cousin tells me my family thought I was bad news. The house is full of rainbow lights, pine needles, lies. I feel like one of those rich kids I used to be jealous of, the ones with so much family they practically spilled through the windows in the living room. Their kitchens were crowded with glossy dishes and medium-rare ribeye steaks, crisp pigs in blankets, cookies oozing with chocolate. We ate *empanadas* in foil and my clothing was full of holes. I don't know where the scars went. I guess what I'm trying to say is this. I smile and eat margherita pizza and think about all the times I could have died and didn't.

Sorry I cried at dinner; do you still think I'm hot?

Yo sé que tú nunca vas a leer este so I'm going to address it to you, I hope that's okay. There's got to be another way, but I have yet to figure it out. What I'm trying to say is I relapsed again. I know what you're thinking—but what about healing? What about laying in fields, burning matches to fingertips, we shared grapes, and everything was a laugh. Feed me and tell me I'm the most hilarious person in your life! Don't think I'll be able to leave this space so please, *quédate.* It's going to happen again; can I count on you to arrive with a mason jar of apple juice? Can you make me toast in dawn? None of this it-will-be-okay then oh-no-it-won't. *¿Tu vistes eso?* The way the pipes were blushing with purple-pink light, we were submerged, the rest of the world bled away—anyways, sorry about the blood, I wish it wasn't mine—and people kept telling me my bandages made me look silly. Here's the thing. *¡Necesito que tu óigame! Necesito* more bread, easy amber ales, champagne but pause the toast to announce to everyone you're not walking out, the only way you'll ever leave is if gators crawl from the swamps and tell you *te vas, necesito amor, necesito* forgiveness and honesty and honestly, please be kind to me. Been trying not to hand away the past like confetti but the floor is covered in trans-

lucent rainbow hexagons and all the butterflies rep-
resent my ex-girlfriends. I look at dinner in front of
me, but my stomach is a pit. Someone sings on the
stage and all I think about are horses. What I mean
to say is I'm daydreaming about the lucky horse-
shoe hanging above my late grandfather's doorway.
I meant I'm thinking about sugar spiders and glass
webs, friends and phrases, no that's not quite right,
rocks in my mouth, shards in the hand again. What
is it I'm trying to say? Thought about excusing myself to the restroom to throw up. *Pensé de tí* and like,
I'm so freaking sorry about that it's not even *chistoso.*
Pero, what is funny these days? So sick of the scars.
So sick of being sick of my ill little stomach. Meant
I'm thinking about putting myself in a small box
and asking you to seal it with postal tape. Meant I'm
thinking about la-la. Ribbon of pesto through the
hottest cheese, want to eat the knife, want the rain to
return and wash me into the drain. To be clear, what
I'm trying to say is *ostra, nuestra vida es complicado,*
told you I'd stop with the jokes but here I am, trying
to tell you about menthol, rolls, herbs, water, pipe,
birds, and even death. Truly, this is about the time
I tried. Mentioned it earlier, on the grass. He's up
ahead—doesn't remember. *Los amo a todos ustedes*
too much. *Vaya a comer,* they said. *Tú es tonta,* they
said. I'm tired of being tired. Please ignore the pleas.
Please turn me into the little crescent moon in the

corner of your phone.

Oignon Brûlé

1.

You arrive at the greenhouse past midnight to pur-
chase vegetables for the *confit*. The day hasn't begun,
you bear a lantern in one hand, emptied seafood
bin in the other. The nursery smells sweet, the only
sound your hands hooking light to the wall, hair falling in front of your right eye, hush of cotton pants
creasing as you bend to pluck mustard greens. Too
soon night will end, you'll appear, bleary-eyed and
covered in soot, ready for the menu. Your attitude
problem is better this way—who wouldn't love you
half-asleep in striped pants, lost the buttons on your
coat, your tattoos are fading and only the bartender
touches the small of your back?

2.

Lace and lettuce, cool weather bundled the peas, the
fields beyond reach a precipice of forests whose hills
become slopes, dips of mud, a root-infested path
overlooking the lake. Mourning doves shouldn't be
awake, but they are. There are howls, bug clicks, the
entrance door swinging gently open and closed from
the wind. You think you'll see her, but she's gone,
turned into a breeze, her petunias have died, her eyes
are deep and bottle-green onions, *Perna canaliculus*

the color of a field in your dreams, you remember she used to tell you bivalves were hearts, she slept with a bucket of clams near her bed, she has gone again, she might be back. One never knows when it comes to Manhattan.

3.

Enough with mozzarella water shots, no twists left so it's time to honey-glue seeds to pear galette glass, you're the underdog, the best sous chef, eating shallot-coated sourdough thinking it might save you but you want it to be her, please say you didn't forget the feeling of shoulders brushing at dinner, please heal, reveal the true color of your irises, you're no good regardless but you'll put on a show. Been writing to her and her alone, she knows you understand, it's New York City baby and all hearts are coated in neon light. You don't know who will replace you, you are hell-born, evening horse, gliding through a twenty-top and stuffing money under cushions, you love hot spoons, new spatulas, you have a special scope for ambition, you're best at the three-plate carry, you tell her you still want to be friends.

4.

I am in the dry storage labeling jars of beans and weeds when you enter. *Long night*, you say, laughing in that brassy way of yours. *There's never enough cof-*

fee, I reply, inhaling the needle-scent of permanent marker. I draw circles on my palm, hoping it will stop my feelings from leaping out of my mouth and into your ears. You smirk as you leave the room; I hope we have the same smoke break.

5.

Distorted garbage cans stand navy-purple in the flood lamps. The air smells of nearby ocean, vanilla scones, old spaghetti, plastic. You sit on the stoop, hair pulled back with a lettuce rubber band. I lean over the railing. Our exhalations become one ghost weighed down by rain, and soon the storm will knit until everything is wet and warm as soil.

Mint Winter Egg

Enchanter's herb and *datura* line the archway above the table. Some of us remark at the algae blooms in the indoor pond, the balcony filled with small silver fish, servers who sidestep each other with ease, we want to let the kitchen know we can cook, too, we can withstand the burn and the hum, we have figured out the thrill that comes with a good four-plate carry, though one of us sprained our thumbs but that's beside the point. We are sitting down to dinner and trying not to flirt with each other, this dinner is about business, this business is about to rewrite the menu, which is almost as thrilling as putting out a good front (or so we like to tell ourselves). Lost in the idea book, our hands smudge ink, write nonsense in the margins.

Someone has drawn a smiley face next to a recipe for a *roux*, we notice some of us have dressed up in gold and deep tones, others wear royal blue blazers even though our kitchen colors are green and red, but why not love the sea, why can't we be multidimensional? We have wants, too, and secrets and recipes never dared in our wildest dreams. Out back, the kitchen prepares our food, someone spills coffee on another server, we understand, we've all been there before.

Soon someone's hand finds another's beneath the table, a new alliance twists, martinis the color of rivers are half-empty, half-full of blueberries, there are martinis garnished with grey-smoke candy canes and the onion rings are bristling with golden crumbs. We are struggling, we miss each other even when we're during one collective presence, cold restaurant, many messes, and perhaps a few broken hearts. We don't call her; she's told us most days are zombie status and living beyond forty-second street has turned her lungs calloused. But if she'd let us, we'd put up lighted wreaths, kiss cheeks, do whatever it took, maybe even forgive the fallout from a bad lagoon-deep love. Who knows? Sometimes our knives make awful sounds on the plates, and we still care for each other.

When it's time for dessert, we are enamored with mint chocolate eggs coated in snowflake sugar; we are so tightly woven together we forget to go home separately, we head to the executive chef's house and fall asleep in the living room, chef jackets crumpled in the corner, there are too many blankets, and the heat is out of control but at least we'll all be on time for work the next day. And when daylight arrives, we march to work in slush, we're very chatty this Tuesday. Maybe it's the love, maybe it's the winter treats, maybe it's a rumor that she's coming back for a visit, and we don't say this out loud, but we wouldn't be able to stay gone, either. There are dreams we'll never chase for fear of breaking apart like old dough, and the harder we work, the less it hurts, tears turning into glittering eyeliner as we take turns grieving in the walk-in freezer. Amongst the sorbets and ice-creams are boxes of fresh, unwashed glassware—we press the wine and whiskey glasses to our cheeks to calm the heat, but once we return to the kitchen we remember, and the ache runs deep and wide as a trench.

2. Monsters

When the woman you have a crush on asks you to host a séance, you say yes

You stained the coffee mug with your lipstick, you walked hand-in-dangerous-hand across the navy-green lawn, October was an anxiety, and it crawled across your skin. Later in the dorms, she suggests you light the candles for the séance. If you close your eyes, it's like she's no longer right in front of you, twisting your dreams up into a knot. She asks what's wrong but even if you tried, you'd never know where to begin explaining that the ache, deep to begin with, has begun to permeate your ribs. *This isn't an Adam thing, but it could be,* she says, gesturing to a scar on her stomach where another tried to surgically re-move some of her bones for a spell. *Did it work?* I ask. *You're here aren't you*—she says, barely able to finish the joke before her mouth opens wide in laughter.

You're not sure if you're sleepy or uncomfortable, if your heart is stopping every few seconds by your hand or hers, there is something rotten about being mortal and even this crush-love—the kind to swal-low you whole, if you let it—won't last beyond the first incision, kiss, stage, orange leaf crunch, then it's going to be blizzard, *I never loved you,* someone else's coat around your shoulders and your neck empty of hands but even in the absence you feel fingers tickling your hairline. Maybe there were ghosts all along, you should have known when you entered the library and the shadows draped their bodies across the walls like your grandmother's coat room and you thought to yourself, for a split second, *is she here right now, witnessing me?* But you shake away the thought, like you always do, and there she is, this woman in a turtleneck with eyes like gemstones asking if you'd like a sip of her coffee. She pokes at the bruise on your hand (from the time you accidentally smacked into a machine in the science department—and who knew what purpose it served, all you knew was that it hurt) and she keeps squeezing each of your fingertips like they might pop off at any second, doll-parts no longer girl-parts, and grief twisted into a storm outside stained-glass windows.

And anyways, what good are scars you can't share, now she's handing you the knife for the ritual and you take it, the heavy golden thing, cradling its hilt like a dangerous rabbit or a bar of sculpted butter, she says if you're not up for the task she can hurt you, but you know from stories it has to be your hand against your own hand, who knows what kind of jaws might escape the floor if you forfeit the blade? You remember suddenly what you had to tell her that day, that you couldn't figure out her eye color, first it was hurricane and then dew-coated lawn, sometimes you dreamed of fire and she was there with coals in her arms and whispers twisting around your head like a suffocation, *I'm thinking about you,* she's saying over and over again until you wake up half-breathing only to find the comforter has gotten on your face again. Now, with the afterlife so close you can practically hear it knocking from floor one, you wonder who put the comforter over your eyes. Is your grandmother disappointed? Is the devil arriving, gently at first, then shudders and cacophony and beautiful lightning, bringing promises and pieces of cake full of pearl seeds? *We could fix each other;* you find yourself saying. We don't need to call up the old gods for this task. *What are you talking about? I don't need you to fix me.* And it becomes an echo in your head, not a soft blossom like you'd hoped, *I don't need you, I don't need you, fix me, fix me,* whose side are you on, just press the knife into your palm for goodness' sake.

After you're done, you know you'll always remember this moment. The way the floor creaked open like a yawn, and hands were reaching out—for her, first, and then you—that's not quite right. It was *she* who reached out for *you,* as if to say *Come with me,* and you did—you, reckless, you, grabbing onto her hand like she was a lifeline instead of a death sentence, you plunged depths both gorgeous and pressing, the air turned to velvet and smoke, when you collapsed on a muddy forest floor you were tangled in each other, laughing, and she took your face in her hands and kissed, smearing palm-blood on your cheek and laughing, *We need some bandages,* she said. All around stood demons whose forms you couldn't even try to recount if you tried, perhaps they wouldn't want you to explain yourself, even now as you trudge through the layers of Hell together, you feel the succession of longing that led to this precious moment, you're alone but at what cost, she tasted like raspberries or was it blood, is she trying to get out of here or is she trying to get you out of here? It's hard to speak.

When the false moon appears, months from now, only one of you will be able to return to the world of the humans, the other will get pushed further into hell. You wonder who will do the pushing, the tugging, the screaming. Let's adjust that thought away. For now, the vampire deer are in the pastures, and she is so beautiful with earrings full of smacking flames and teeth getting sharper by the day. What a blessing, to know she's strong enough to devour your heart in a single bite, and you'd still live but at what cost, but damn the cost, maybe she deserves the fire, and you deserve nothing.

Nobody

Can't tell this story without erasing part of myself, can't tell you I went to the woods to find you and found the paths not empty but filled with oak leaves, red from Fall, like so many puddles of blood, would you still want to kiss me if you knew, kiss me there, impress upon the hurting space with the healing space, give me a year of Sundays, sunbursts, lemon mint and sea oats, the thing about the name is it tells a story, but you don't care, French mulberries have nothing on the sweetness of your smile, hazel wine and blanketflower, I want to save you but I haven't figured out how yet to save myself, but want you, plain, in the kitchen in your tie, maybe at the stove with your soft cotton pants, the others have left, perhaps a few mill around the gardens outside, when we near each other by the fridge all they'll see is a pair of friends having a casual discussion about jars of milk, won't see inner cheek bite, leap of the heart, loss of faith, pain like a bear's tooth lodged deep in the muddy leak of my heart, it hurts a little bit to stand so close to you, I've always wondered about the reindeer and the hoof tricks, not enough stories in bars, not much time remains before we'll never see each other again, so what now, little royal catchfly, are you so clever, are you going to stay after winter twists your muzzle in ink and the unforgiving small gods take away your name, your status, your bacterial culture, doesn't matter, you don't want me to help you, that much has been made clear, you will never call me mouse ears, you will never bow after the torches have been extinguished, there is always gasoline in the house, everything heat and heart, not about lips or touch, but what does it matter, even if I revealed to you the risk and the hickory, the sour and the wounds, little bumps from the sun, this crush is crushing, unkind, little smolder in the bonfire out back, my risk, my candle, soon they find us stooped in cold light, someone asks what you're up to, looking for leftover sweetness, is all you say before you wink, stitch of your name oozed blue on my lungs.

Macaw

Unwell. You pull the tail off your own body. Melt. Walk straight into forest. In your mind, the moon has already left. The theories you have of yourself are wrong. In school, you are a chicken. You eat your stomach during dinner. No one notices you wear your past like a cloak, but everyone notices you're scared. You're alive and then you're passing out during your own inner monologue. Have you ever really known what it means to be earnest? Will you be able to ignore natural judgement? Why do you think you matter so much? Why do you hang out with the boy who smokes at the top of the garage? His faded converse sneakers have song lyrics and ex-girlfriends' names scrawled on the sides. You make out in a forest sticky with bugs and June. When you were younger you lied. Now you are older and building little houses around your trauma. Every day your little houses are eaten by wolves, and you are also a wolf. Your father lied. Your mother says you inherited this trait from him. He never tried to stop you when she called him crying. You weren't successful. Are you really living, now? The bedsheets were blue then red. Everything was a hot stone in your head. All your veins are gathered at your center, and they pump your heart wrong. You are a wolf and then you tear yourself into wolves. You never learned lessons. What if everyone leaves? How can you learn to be a better dog, build a better house, avoid eating yourself alive each night? You are tired of metaphor, of self-harm, of the poem of your body. Your ex-crush can feel you filling the room with a toxicity. You ask him if this is a story yet and he shrugs before turning into a company of parrots.

A history of what happened

There existed a progression of long nights where you woke in the middle of sometime and sat on someone else's floor. It was always sticky. There would come a numbness, but first there would come hot pain. You'd think to yourself, *this is happening to me,* but you didn't have words like *why.* It was difficult to go swimming. You followed people to the woods and slept in the backs of trucks and you hated the smell of cologne, cigarettes, beer, weed. There persisted a sticky-sweet quality about a man who had driven all that way just to hurt you. No one brought you to the hospital and your mother was pissed off, not sad, when she found out you wanted to die. A stickiness about the gauze and the cause for it all was what happened. Back then, you were so bright. God, do you remember ash and gummy worms? There were holes in your pants so big people could see the scars on your knees and then some. You stole from other mothers. You took pregnancy tests and bought rolls of bandages. You were slick in the night, hanging out the windows of cars, men called you *baby,* and your teachers told you it was all your fault. It's like you want to tell this story but when you look back the memories are slippery, your body is a ceiling ghost, on the surface of the bed grows a mold, you can't see

what happened anymore, you grasp at sea foam and
then you slide, like water, through your own fingertips.

The Saint

You knew you were in love the first day of winter on the beach. Cold surf, his wife ahead with golden retrievers who wouldn't stop barking at seals, her scarf bright and red as a blood blister, black hair tied back in a neat bun, your friends on either side of her, the two of you walking slowly behind. You knew you weren't supposed to be alone together, not after she found you whispering over an old photo album from his teenage years when he and his friends dressed up as different saints reenacting biblical events. There were his hands, shakily captured in the moonlight, mid-prayer. His ex-girlfriend, eating macaroni with lump crab, grinning as a poorly made halo tilted off her head, its surface coated in tinfoil.

Everyone was holy, back then, he was saying, and we all made wings out of newspaper and super glue. I'd always wished to be a saint.

She cleared her throat in the doorway and the two of you separated, unaware any distance had been eaten in the first place, everything warm and amber as grilled lemon rinds.

Or perhaps you knew over dinner, when she sat him

next to you, the rest of the faculty devouring their flank steaks and scallops, the dean of translation studies joking about taking pomegranate glaze shots, short ribs and enoki mushrooms, someone brought horseradish cream, someone made mussels with tomatoes, potatoes, and deep green brine. There were words embossed on the forks and the knives, your silverware reading *Seeds and Butter*, the inner curve of his steak knife bearing *Beg, Mercy, Hurt*. The beef Wellington bleeding out of its doughy case, red peppers belly-up in the moonlight, everyone wearing duck boots, everyone from Boston.

You're making a fine addition to the English department, she said, bright white teeth biting into baby beets and in that moment, you knew she'd never been without money, never needed the dentist, she probably never got chicken pox or ran out of breath when she exercised.

I'm grateful to be here, you replied, unsure why you were talking about this now, late January, when months had gone by with meetings and wine, chopped blackberries and her gaze at your back.

You were tender, you were his rib straight from his empty stomach, constantly filled with sadness, always pining after the wrong person.

Thank God we finally hired someone who publishes literature, he said.

At this, his wife frowned, pushed parmesan around her plate. You wondered why she didn't eat the eggplant and get the insults over with. Instead, she asked you for a hand in the kitchen. His fingers, warm on your thigh, illicit touch beneath the table, your colleagues staring at you like you were a reincarnated rabbit they'd killed earlier in the road, everyone with roast-you gaze, wanting to turn your body into portabello pot roast, seafood *cioppino*, another excuse to drink.

Her kitchen was summertime. Dried leaves woven throughout the ceiling, dishes printed with surf curls and sand dollar discs, a spider having survived New Year's Eve scuttled above your head.

I'm sorry about what happened to you.

You wondered what she was talking about before realizing she'd been reading your memoir. You can see her now: glasses on the bridge of her nose, body slouched in her father's armchair, pieces of your memoir printed on colorful paper, particularly resonant lines covered in circles, strikethroughs, question marks. She made her way through the early years, the violence in the old barns, the forests which threatened to swallow you whole, your mother who told you to die.

I don't know what you mean, specifically. As in, *dare.* As in, *say it.* The words, the happenstance, the violence with many names.

She took a step closer; you wondered what you must look like to the others. Two women in *North Face* jackets with stain-free blue jeans, amber duck boots, one blonde and the other raven-haired. Her hand on the side of your face. From the outside of the kitchen, she seemed gentle. Caress from an older faculty member, a woman, as if to say, been there, screwed him. Destroyed lives before you even set foot on this campus, ruined jaw bones before, everyone knows a professor is a witch in hiding. They don't see the way she grips, digging her red nails into your flesh. These are the same nails your mother had. You want to ask her about mirrors, but think better of it, knowing your mother wouldn't stop digging until she reached blood, bone, gauzy human mucus. Best not to offer ideas. How tired you were back then. You'd do anything to stop her.

I know, she replies, and you turn the phrase over in your head like shards of caramel.

She knows about your crush-love, she knows your mother grabbed your jaw, she knows about the pain, all of it. But when you open your mouth, you find a rubbery straw instead. You are a spider in her palm, many legs, violet body, a party trick, a punishment. You see with your many eyes you, seated at the table, his hands around a newly uncorked bottle of Cabernet Sauvignon, a version of you waving in the air as you tell jokes about your absent father, everyone comments your backstory is *hilarious*.

After dinner, he'll find you in the kitchen, just hanging out on the lip of the counter. He takes you into his hand and again you think about the fragility of animals, bugs, creatures, plants in the garden whose stems you ripped out of the ground, a yolk-yellow marble you once swallowed, broken teeth and even more broken boys. He apologizes for his wife's behavior, explains things are better this way. He takes a mason jar off the shelf, its body fluted and grey, drops you inside. Dip of a scissor and soon there are three breathing holes at the top and you at the bottom, hungry for the day someone accidentally opens the lid.

Ache

Your taste in music makes you cute / you feel a deep thrum / decayed flowers grow / he's near so you hide behind a lamp / but soon, you are a lamp / too bright / frilled sleeves / alcohol in your glass the color of the sun / kind of beautiful / the way longing twists into a tarp / folds your lungs into a box / you pretend to be reluctant when really / mouth bite / dental blood / hungrier than before / heat / there comes a patience / your ex offers you lemons crusted with sugar / you are exceptionally nervous in the corner in the room / are you being as truthful as you could possibly be / are you missing the holler / little spider in the back of your throat / electric dress / don't look at his pants / take the moon from the sky / offer your bones to the old gods / watch as he remembers your freckles / his new girlfriend has glasses / you consider breaking them / you consider how tangible the inside of your heart has become / space closes / strawberries dipped in frosting / too much swearing / nothing else to say / except this / her purse is patterned with glittering jelly jars / *okay Lisa Frank* / but secretly you'd give up your veins to feel his touch again / she teases you / maybe this could be easy / why can't you designate your heart to many at a time / why the judgement / you three could be early mornings / reading a dogeared copy of *A Moveable Feast* / the more the merrier / the more you become a writer / half-naked legs under the table / he takes your drink / she offers you cake / this is someone else's party / and by the way / you never said you weren't selfish / this is about hunger / this / my dear / is about lying.

Sirens are mermaids with knives

The sea is full of promises, aquatic foxes, a platform for starfish to feed, the seabed is warm, tinged blue from lack of light but we are bright with our lamps and bulbs, mother pinched us like a lobster might try to hold the hand of an all-consuming rope net, she said we were tidal waves, she said we were boring, she told us stories about how love lives in the groundwater and we believed her, so we're out with our silence and our feelings, you know how it is, the frazil ice isn't a bother, sorry about the iris rumor and how we snuffed out the crown, do you know what we are, do you know how to flee, do you see the skeletons of sailors all moldy and green by the base of the tree, nature is a basin of worship, we string words together like we string paste candies on a dancer's necklace, things are unstable but at least we know how to write.

How many fish did mother want, we wonder, we wander beneath an uneven sky, everything is silt and soft, left a salt apple with all its teeth, left you even though we shouldn't have, but what would life have been like if we'd stayed? Sure, there'd be cable knit sweaters and an amber kitchen, you would have known what to do when the whale beached itself on the shore, you wore wire rims and had a fake gold tooth, your name rhymes with words like *potato* and *tectonic plate*, you tried to keep hurricanes in jars but everything fell apart until your house was covered in glass shards, what a mistake to tell us about the electricity and the fast ice, but we digress, you're gone and we're busy with the sea.

Everything sings down here and the dolphins have a swearing problem, mother wouldn't approve, she waits up for us at the mouth of Ocean House, prays we'll become fossils she can hang above the fireplace, she fights with her sister and wears high heels in the sandbars, well whatever, what do we know of helmets and eggs and fins, but jesus christ was your anger a problem and you said you didn't care about the house of violence, tried to make us give up fishing and food, we even broke up with shrimp, there are no lovers at the bottom of the trench but it is quite nice to trade stories with frilled sharks.

It's like we told you, we're not done until we've overturned every sand dollar and revealed all we have to offer, flip, here another secret, another secret, another secret, a patch of blood, it's not our responsibility to make you feel it, flip then jaws, claw, tentacle wing, sorry-sorry stamped in the coral barnacles and we'll never be in love again but it doesn't matter, the degree to which we'll swim to preserve ourselves is

extreme and there lurk the hearts, all ruby and bio-
luminescent in the pitch cold dark, it's too late for
dreams of tomatoes and aster, what happens with
the knife stays on the knife, one by one we pull apart
with our teeth the unstable atrium, the deceptive
aorta, the right to have a ventricle, here comes the
knife, the daughters, the light.

Pycnogonid

Things get sour when we're dyeing each other's hair tangerine in your mother's bathroom. There are ibis statues everywhere, the ceiling is coated in rubbery leaves bought at estate sales, sometimes when I enter your world it's hard to figure out what's real and what's reflection, who is the double and is the oil painting coming to life to strangle me in my sleep or what, and why are all your father's shoes lined up at the back of the house, everyone knows he's never coming back, went to bargain for the last jug of milk in town and the witch laced his heart into her own, they dragged each other to the ocean and argued until they sank the ship, your mother doesn't care, she lines the shoes up by color, she lets spiders wrap nests in their husks, she feeds the spiders sugar and each of their webby beds is glistening in the last light of the season.

Just a few hours ago we were running through the backyard, I was on your shoulders, and you were laughing so hard I thought you were going to choke, we were making pinky promises and screaming in fairy circles, you found a mushroom that looked just like a marble you had as a kid and instead of keeping it for yourself you gave it to me. This color is all wrong, I can hear you saying. But I'm wondering if the hair dye is wrong or if it's that you're starting to look like me.

You never wanted a twin, would have preferred to walk through the sandy patches by yourself, that summer I saw you drowning in shallow water and I helped you away from the crabs whose arms were securing you to the sand, some of the crabs were playing you songs on miniature flutes they'd made from discarded beer bottles and other crabs still were crying but I took you anyway, this isn't a mermaid thing, everyone in your family is sour and salty, everyone wears bras with starfish stamped across their surfaces and you're the worst at swimming, you're the best at holding me in your arms, your mother should be my mother.

You're so pissed off about the orange situation you don't notice me slipping into your life, easy there, double-bubble gum and double down on the trouble, no longer girl but copy, I am pretending to be you at the dining room table and your mother is serenading me while making pancakes, they'll never find out you're still in the bathroom, you've shrunk to the size of a fish in the tub and soon you'll be gilded and edgy like a star, do I want seconds? Your mother is asking. I do, I do, I reply, I am her second-best, no longer useless, but I will miss the way we used to lay on the grass together and eat sticky buns, those nights we wore your father's yellow rainboots and the land was warm and misty from July, you said something like no one was as nice as me and I thought, for a split second, about what might happen if I didn't devour your whole.

Fisher's Affair

I know you're hiding her in the bathtub, turquoise and jaw bones, seaweed hair, fins, reefs, navy blue hearts, thought you said you were done with secrets. After we left the forest, and you were so tired, I helped rip arrows from your back, I watched you fall apart, whale wine and bone snickers, a hot tub filled with sand, promised you'd give up the water and weather and blue. I'm sure she loves you, thinking about your neon eyes while she combs waxy dragonflies from her hair, I wonder if she marvels when light catches in the room, is she strength, is she singing in your bathtub, does her perfume glow florescent on your collarbone, magic and moons, eyes bottle and hunter green, I thought you said I was your lake of desires. Your anger storms and acid splash, ache of rain on Tuesday roofs, hot gold knife and home of lilies, I possessed frogs for you, made the mold flush from love letters, now lost, left the house, stained my jacket tripping over roots, I'm running after lost shadows, but I haven't lost quite yet, I'm still here, a poltergeist prowling among the cherry patches.

Back when the deer were horses, and the horses were rivers

The air filling with blue smoke and blue horses whose breath stokes the kindling, hooves upturning earth, they're running again through the streets and the back road paths, towards your house with the faded wisteria creep, lilac and amber in the rainstorm and you're running out of cigarettes, left your car window open again and someone's cat has climbed inside, warm and soft red seats reminiscent of a heart, how many times we'll walk next to each other through the pines before your heart turns and burns into a crisp in the bonfire, your friends are cooler than me, wearing gold bead bracelets necklaces layered and chokers coated in crescent moons, well-water used to reflect my eyes, now everything is green, soft as satin goes, your faded elbows in your late father's coat, I pretend to be your mother in the dim light of the kitchen, I am your sister and brother, too, your cat with the tuxedo fur, I am the company you keep, the worry at the back of your neck, we reach the deck close to dawn, the horses have turned into swans with blue feathers and algae-coated beaks, did you know the willow tree is an ecosystem feeding the edges of town how long until you tell me you don't love me anymore, who do I think I am easy to be cared for,

am I the host, maybe hound with its muzzle dipped
in the ground, problems with teeth at my neck and
my back memorizes the bark of a tree we extinguish
the farmer's candle gardens, we climb the roof, we
are daring and young and chain-smoking deep into
Saturday I wish then daylight was around for long
enough to save my life.

I wish I could outrun the river, become soft and se-
dated the kind of being you'd leave and think, *they'll
make it on their own, their body fits perfectly into the
doorway of evening* and when I finally disappear, all
those years later, will you remember to write to me,
will you read my letters, here's another, I try to reach
back through the legs and the haze, can you hear me
across ribcages and dry ice, buckets of headlights
broken and collected at the side of the road, amber
rings the dead deer's head in a helmet, hooves so similar to that of a horse, antlers shaking and coated in
beads, I am reminded of the women, I am reminded
of the wounds, the city with its stretches then hums
when my family was still alive they would wave at me
out the balcony of the fourth floor, crying and letting
go of their satin handkerchiefs, the expensive kind,
tucked away in the pockets of guests and mourners,
we are at the funeral for the animals, I want to trick
myself into shrinking, I want to run across tracks and
turn into a dragonfly, maybe a rope, a promise, a crate

of oranges and peaches, messy and blessed as flesh, sour, stings the place where you insert the dagger, this isn't a song or a secret tossed between ex-friends, this is my life force perched on the edge of your window-sill, this is me clawing at the phone booth doors, I'm already raging and ready to race, cross stables fields of blooms, say it, how you prefer ravishing gardenias, even if I wanted to would I curb my face, cure the heat, sticky flip-flops of my youth discarded beneath plastic lawn chairs, we throw streamers at the party, eat meat down to the bone, stay up too late, do I tell you I miss you or do we collect smooth wet rocks and small seashells discarded from the mussel mud, must I sculpt the altar by myself?

I don't know how to make a priest out of squirrel jaws and telephone wires and we all grieve them, the deer with their stories and points and stars, but no one knows the real reason they keep running out into the road, even though there is a history of danger and hitting, there is a consolation prize there is sorry-sorry, a loss space inhabited by flower bearers and a bishop from the next town over, his heart is a chamber where hide liquids and bottle caps, enraptured cats, an entire arboretum and then some, then we have to say goodbye to the horses, someone must braid their manes, someone must take out the screws, soon we are singing and losing, I am drying my veins out like frog rocks, you once told me to save my life, I couldn't protect you even if I tried to tear down the ribbons at the intersection of the statues, so many words for *sea* and *moon*, not enough for *loss* or *carve* my dear, save the bones for me, save your prayers, your shawls, your sorries, I will slip in the secret space of love, I will rest until the earth turns green and hot, screw the evidence, save me the ashes from the rites, remind me that I can survive tough stuff, violence and such is the crown on the head of the eldest buck, all red stains but whose car was it and what happened to the river water, where do I return when the lights go out and the barn is sealed?

The softer the orange, the tastier the gold

There is a horse running across the field. I take off my glasses and its form becomes a storm cloud. I wake; you might not love me, but we head down to the kitchen together, your pajamas snagging on old stairs, my hand steadying myself as I pretend to be another person. At breakfast we control the pull and rush of others, though I can't see your face behind a stack of toast, I know we'll snap together, fast magnets, back again but we don't really care about details, back again but why do we always do this, back in those days I turned my imagination into something you could shatter, I let your words open blooms on my skin, I was a scab, I lost my nerve and my scarf and my scars in the squishy sun patches of October. You'd laugh if you knew how much I was trying. A riotous joy in your half-asleep eyes, I'm trying not to try, I'm trying to fold my body into the snack cupboard, I'd rather be a chain link on a cat collar, I'd rather tell lies, tell me this: did you forget about the fires and the forests, the gristmill and the gods and the ground beef cold between our fingers, a *sala* full of home cooks, a Saturday entrusted with meaning? But what about the way the crows roped across the sky, but what about the sob caught in my throat, but what about your arms?—there's a reason I don't go home anymore. There's a lot you don't know about the inside of my skull, worn away like crabs or time, saltwater hands, bone turns to shell, purple then thin in the sun, a part of me is always intentionally disconnected, a plug yanked out of the wall, this isn't about feelings, nor is it about panic, I have no more heat to share. Mid-day. We warm our hands by the wood stove, we talk about frittatas and blue ducks, geese with their honey spots, a quail the size and gumption of a heart. Someone brings glowing caviar, someone scrambles meat in a pan, someone asks what I'm doing these days, what's going on with that old writing thing, yes I remember something like that, the direction of the pen in my hand, but already the conversation is glossy glaze-haze then ham, someone asks for the jelly, you're killing me with the anterior exam, the tendon twist, screw the ulna, what would I even know about the fade out, I could be a poltergeist walking and you'd never notice, not when food jumps through me clear, not when I can't stay in the tub, not later, not sooner, not ever, not anyone but you.

Prism

1.

You want to take my hand in the bird room, you want black coffee and for forgiveness to feel like a rush in your cheeks. It's all chic desire and double macaw beaks, they've even stuffed butterfly stomachs, their wings are smudges of amaranth and gamboge, I'm celadon from low-hanging lamps in the skeleton hall, velvet walls, I wonder why these bones aren't in cases. With each turning of the season the elemental witch arrives to polish the displays, her forest magic accidentally bringing everything to life—*For One Night Only*—read the neon signs. You wanted to see canaries in flight, you wanted to know if gemstones make their way back to each other, it's winter and my heart is falling apart. I'm distracted by your ex, newly arrived in a jumpsuit and no less than ten studs in one ear, she's purchasing candy filled with fake eyes, she's making her way towards plastic trees whose trunks lean in the direction of her brilliance.

2.

Splash glass fragments and *liopleurodon* smirks, it's not that I needed protection, just wanted more cases to break, all the shatter is sugar and anyway, you always told me you liked the way my heels crunch on broken surfaces. But I'm alone as I pass the fish, she's got you in conversation about crocodiles with phlox claws, I'm distracted by the curves of ancient creatures, wish I were gorgeous first, vicious second, but these days I'm all cigar-smoke and attitude, I don't like how everyone has stories of you and some teeth display keeps mocking me, *jealous, baby, jealous,* but I'm a bandaged goddess and I don't need my face where I'm going next.

3.

Cervalces Scotti amble through stormwaters, pincushion moss bundles, there are sphagnales, there is java and beautiful diatom, an entire display of spoon leaved moss made of child's play mold spelling out *warning me,* I glance at the witch, wonder if she could twist someone into an elemental trap, but she's busy, her nose in a whiskey. She shrugs when I see the greens are mimicking conversations of the guests, the walls of the West Wing are all *eyes* and *clutter* and come back then *twice I tried but I'm no good at the game.* I want to sleep all month only to wake for her touch, want to be a twice-bloomed horse flower, and my hair could be hook-hued, nails as hoof, I'm lost in all my want, I don't find out she's with you in the tiger exhibit until much, much later.

4.

I wasn't there when your dreams came to die. As a curator, I was young, I always had California on my mind and I thought I'd already buried myself in your heart, you had my name tattooed on your hip, whose idea this was I can't recall and when you asked me to do the same I said no, you only get to carry a knife of prayer once in your life, plus I still hadn't gotten over my ex. Back then I ate breakfast on the commute to work, I spent hours commissioning one hundred artists to make pieces based solely on the prompt *Angel* and nights I came home covered in feathers and hickeys, you loved that I was good in bed even though I wasn't charming when I had coffee. My head filled with gutter spiders, I was pacified by your hands, but you tried to tattoo my fingernails when I wasn't looking, and I guess I haven't forgiven you since.

5.

Again, why are you mad at me when you're the one who cheated first? You said she was a blue jay; you slurred your words and cursed me for being an old punchline. I responded by purchasing a dozen paintings of women in snow wearing masks of bees, each expensive scene filled with hips and hands, spreads of semi-perfect oil rivers, except one corner of each canvas, where a jagged knife-hole rests from when you tried target practice while my back was turned. I asked if you missed the older gods and you shrugged, turning into a fox, and sneaking into an empty shoebox before I had a chance to yell at you about the scars.

6.

There are glowsticks in the courtyard and college students toying with a half-dipped golden piano. We're all stuck here until the spell wears off so I guess I'll have something to eat, it's kind of difficult when suits of armor keep getting in the way, that and this drunk girl who won't stop calling me *Honey*, she thinks I'm cool, she's unaware I'm wasting away enshrined in a contract with a young god who lays lambs at my feet but he won't have sex with me at the altar and everything feels like a waste of time.

7.

There's an animal I've never seen before walking down the employees-only hall. I don't know where you went. Instead of wasting away, I decide to follow. The animal commands many tails and eyes, long black ears like a rabbit, each paw has soft barbs at the end, each time I touch its hide it becomes ticklish. Down the hall we go, past preservation rooms, stacks of picture frames waiting hungrily for wings and pins, someone's stolen the moon and tied it to the back room, there are employee lockers filled with candy and a shawl eerily familiar to the one my grandmother owned, stenciled with sugar birds and coiled chicken feet. At the end of the hall, we reach an empty doorway. The creature waits for me, so we exit side-by-side. My stomach drops and keeps on falling. The next day I awake as a silver-lilac knife tied to a string in a case of other shining ones. When night falls and the witch arrives, she carefully instructs me how to aim for your heart.

Sorry

For carrying the ghost around this long. Nineteen years weep into twenty. You're still bleeding, wondering when dreaming turned into exhaustion. Someone comes to pick you up during a snowstorm and you find yourself crying in the back of the car, thinking about what you really shouldn't be thinking about. And everyone knows it, how you're broken. Though it's close to four in the morning, you wear sunglasses and try not to imagine the car sliding on half-melted snow, its sleek body tumbling like an ice chunk into a nearby building. When you get safely to the airport, you're half-awake, still haunted. Ghosts sift through Boston and follow you all the way to Charlotte. You meet new people soon after, in a place you can't name, and they tell you it won't stop unless you stop it. But the year was sixteen and now it's seventeen and nothing hurts more than when you do it to yourself. You write little pieces about harm. People in your workshop give you looks, or perhaps you're imagining it. At breakfast you think again of blood. You walk to class with itchy skin and worry at the calcium deposits in your flesh. Weeks later, at the doctor, you contemplate saying sorry. Say *sorry, the speculum hurts because of.* Say *sorry, but can you tell where the tissue healed?* Say *long gone.* The circle near your radiocarpal is almost gone and days later you're making another. Nothing stops time. Someone tells you this, too, counts. Your feelings slip away, and you can't find them. Soon, arms. The love is almost too much to bear. Sometimes they help melt loose frazil around your heart, other times you wonder if anyone is impacted by your presence. There's so much to feel. It hurts. When someone asks you what happened you tell them an accident, leave it at that. You wonder if anyone's wondering. You say *sorry about the love, I wish it wasn't mine.*

Sublime

You wake to a road dyed purple from too much rain and a red sun the exact size and shade of your new scar. But soon it will fade, and sixteen turns to seventeen, there are men you're in love with smoking cigarettes on the stoop, your ex-girlfriend is in the kitchen drinking milk with ghost cats, you are a broken thing but that's nothing new. There's no one to save you, not even yourself, you who drove so many times in the middle of the night to meet men with tattoos who only want to shatter you into fragments they can more easily taste. It becomes difficult to say what's going on. Your feelings turn to descriptions of mushrooms and large green leaves. You have a crush but it's so hot it leaves footprints and smears dirt on the flower tiles, your feelings turn into jars of sugar, but don't get it twisted, this is anything but sweet. Nothing hurts like the extra digs, fingers as claws, you want to but you're not going to, and when is this going to end? The others toast. They play records and drink out of glass tumblers. You've sold your grandmother's jewelry to put food on the table but then again, you're also thirty-three and this is a twisted little memory which sits in the center of your being. Then again, all your memories are collaged. What does it matter, how you felt at seventeen, how you feel now, years later? You tell people your age and they make jokes about Christ. You tell people about your problem but can't seem to move beyond words like *emergency* and *issue,* everything dissolves in your mouth, you walk your silence back and truth claws its way out again. There is blood and then there isn't. There is no easy way to tell this story. You leaf through books of poetry and witness other writers being clear. They explain what happened to them in a way you know you'll never be able to achieve. This, too, is hard. You wish to be drunk. You don't miss the house with the sharks and the needles, but then again, sometimes you hang your body out of the car like you're a teenager again, being whisked away on an adventure. When you arrived at those houses, what would your mother have thought, if she really knew what was going on? What would your friends say now, if you told them the truth?

This isn't another story of how we counted money in Hell, but it could be

Raspberries in bowls, you left rhubarb for crusted copper roads, buildings inch together, windows are knives, you hid your city somewhere—will you know how to return after all this fight? Will you sell back the rings, unstitch your name from every band, prick your fingers on keys and leaf points which hang false in the blown glass shop, your exes lurk in doorways and the fly amanita expresses its hunger, lines edges of the street like code, the rugs are bags full of cut candles, the cinnamon store doesn't want you near, the ox tongue is waiting for your touch, this isn't a story of stealing or stealth but it could be a reclamation of love, an un-stamping of faces from coins, but please put slender envelopes in their final resting spots, blow Charon a kiss before crossing the river, your beloved has left town but you'd never know, her earrings dangle like fruits from trees, thought you caught a strand of her hair against clay and brick, an awning made of slick stinkhorn and starfish, there is basket, there is chorus, there is octopus and squid, a crab reaching out at all angles, beautiful poison lesson land, where did you decide to abandon the coral, the wings, plastic covering fire flowers, the outline of her heart as it beats in the machine shop, her leftover bite on the back of your neck, no one cares about the vampiric drama or the dame selling scarlet, wax caps grow and you're almost out of diamonds, and what are we going to do about dinner? This isn't a story about hands, not about chords or ether, the empty cigarette pack you found laced with gems, your tobacco stained jars and the day the lakes crawled back into the sea, you knew you'd never return home again, time—time became the wire fire in the back of a station wagon, the extra jaws you grew just to enter into Hell, and the gasoline lobsters made you lonely, it's not like everyone has a sequined soul, it's not like you're sorry but you're starving, so into the house we go, I'm trailing behind with the hooks, I'm your protection but these days you call me a carnivorous bird, you take backs and shoulder blades into hands and I take badges, bandages, brooches and bricolage, stuffing oil paintings and sapphire peach cores into purses, it's not a finance thing, I hope you understand.

I have a crush on a bog

They dress us with crows, my heart is a glittering on-ion and my veil barely stays on my face, these days are liquid-long, crawling up, desire appears on my windowsill like a many-winged bug, I want to tell you I had a nightmare again last night, that I lost you in grey-green bog water, you disappeared into the mouth of a soft crocodile, told me it wasn't a big deal because you love toothy alphabets, tattoos on your thumbs only, you can come back if you want, bring forth brine bracelets, branches filled with birds whose projects are sequin-focused cross my mind with wicking details, I promise I'll let you talk about raisins. I'll stick my feet in the pond even though I'm scared. We can be here for a few days, a few hours, a few more good years, celebrations will be filled with confetti holographic and green, each shape a beautiful cutout of cranes, carrots, silver fish then sparkling roses, the lovely pale fires we once snuffed out with our sweatshirt sleeves, we can turn memo-ries to stamps, send effort in salt pails, write some love letters, I'll wear your consumer's claws around my neck, I feel home when we're by the shore bark twists, do you feel me watching the water or are you over my crush, but do you want to wear a chandelier, do you want to make the bees jealous, your hair is blush sometimes lobelia cardinalis other days I'm in jeopardy and your crimson birds tell me you like being a ghost, they can hear you out-singing their feelings in early evenings, we miss you but you're busy, no orchid-and-arrow at my back but I can feel you, your aim is perfect your eyes are acorn and gramineus, do you still feel euphoria at the sight of water, do you still hate tentative soil, do you know what a breeze feels like against the back of your neck? For the sake of bogs, the bags, the jersey girls and waiting honey-infused pitchers, do you feel rich now you're digested, do you feel loving now you're a nutrient, have you become a plant tissue, can you stop me crying? It's early spring and I'm reminded of drowsy days when you laced your fingers through the ocean's harness, no Venus yet I'm still trapped, I'm supposed to return home like nothing ever happened, and you're supposed to cast a proper haunting flood, your waters are cranberry bogs and you're appealing to everyone the problem was never your beauty, it was your lack of desire to eat me it was your obsession with left-handed fang protectors, yes that winter I fell in love again, but my heart only knows your name, I accidentally told on myself in the county diner, I'm being hunted by the others and you're not even brave enough to whistle a goodbye my way. I might have been brave once, I might have told you I hate when you grow out of control, you don't care,

you're multiplying rosemary puffs and secret quartz
fox in trap crates you're not tolerant of locks, this is
your zone, my—my caroliniana, please keep the gators at bay, I'll take off my boots before I enter your
sacred waters.

When we break up, I am no longer a mermaid

Each night I head to the forest to hang the stars; I remember you always loved red poison monster flowers and the leafy confetti tossed upon our house after a storm. You loved coffee mugs printed with bugs and those days we believed we were good enough; we were frosted webs and yolky lake jelly, not even vampire bats could tear us apart, yet I came home one smooth-moon evening to find you were gone, in the place of a note you left lake water I remember once you said she came to you in dreams, gauzy-winged and tongue-pierced, I know I'm your disappointment, lost half my magic when I crawled out of the lake but if you recall it was your clever argument about solutions and beer-bottle concussions that led me to leaving in the first place, you took down a fawn for me and swapped my tail for legs. I am a projection of your unending hunger, I am taking the arrows with purple-clover centers and soon no one will hold your jaws in their hands, does she even know how to clean fangs? Perhaps I'll wear your faux-fur blazer, I'll take her feather crown and become a glitter-and-clover infused darling, heart hurts to know you never took the fur to the cleaners I made it for you with threads from froth-lined riverbanks, you told me you only felt powerful with the pleasure that comes with sacrifice and offerings, I bet she doesn't know you have halogen fillings, I heard you two never sleep, I guess it was just another fairytale, a halcyon wrapping pleasure and pain around my fists like boxers' gloves, but I'm sea-dear-girl now, it's going to take a lot more than your fire-claw-bite to chew me up. In the center of the field, I see her, I raise my arrows from the Gods and aim for her heart, she bursts into party streamers, music notes, plush hearts hopping across the yard, did you really fall in love with an enchanted toy, but before I get the chance to ask, you're at my throat pulling me into the underworld, have they really not called off the punishment yet? So here we are, creatures among creatures, old gods and lava sobs, there is gem powder in my hair, and I'm permanently dehydrated but at least we're together.

Instead of telling you the truth I go to the red river

I know you'd rather be in the caverns where bubbled stones encroach, or maybe we could be sculpting wings and hands out of clay. You want to know what's going on but we're in a forest kitchen where flaky pinecones and flowers grow, everything in this life is counterfactual and I am the villain, I gather worshippers who bear conch shells, spotted bonnets and rose hued murex, I remember you were like, *quit writing about science babe and tell the truth for once* but you assume this isn't exactly what happened, that when we sunk to our knees in the water you weren't good or graceful, your memory rewrites your heart until it turns into a knotted felt thread, can you feel my hands were once mycelium rots, my history is harm-full, did you know I thrive in decay? This isn't about kissing or killing or kitchens, this is about details, thorns in brush patches, gods who are also foxes asleep between roots, a tree you name Daphne. Know I'm sorry I'm a monster, even sorrier you said you'd love me anyway, as if you know how to return my unkempt heartbeat into a smooth rhythm, as if you know I'm already on the road to being in love with you, as if you know everything—and you do— before I do, you wake up and the earth reveals its secrets to your ears only. If you were a god, you could save me or you could turn me into a plant. After all, why not? Why can't I reveal myself to you, why can't we do our laundry in the sea again? You're so close to me in the water, I don't tell you I'm afraid of blood, but you *know*, in that gentle way of yours, about openings and stains and frequency. Someday I'll tell you about gloom and clots, someday I'll be better, I'll be unrecognizable. I wonder how we look, so close to each other atop inches of water. Your face so near to mine, I could take it in my hands, I could be your lamp holder, I could stop biting my lip, I could be wicked and witchy and fun. You're gentle, telling me I'm luster and seek. Please excavate the love, take it into a sponge, tell me where the proper place is to end things, that if I leave, you'll not be in a polycule with the furies, please tell me you'll be soft, please don't turn me into a freshwater snack for salt-starved jaws. In this kitchen space again—but is a kitchen really a kitchen if there is nowhere to burn or howl or produce cold rot? I tell you the truth with my back turned. I carve a prayer into the cucumber basin, for my body's metamorphosis from garish and selfish to a goat large enough to die in the sink. Your hands turn me to face you, pinning me with the knife still in my hand, I won't drop it, I'll be careful, breathless, a beautiful lying fling, your mouth is killing me, I wonder where the water has gone. If we were never in the river, why am I still covered in blood?

During which the witches descend into the haunted house together

If you're fine with the decay, we can be remarkable. I tell you about the architecture which consumes my mind, and you think I'm so smooth, how could a house follow someone so far out into fields where abandoned wells stand, dotting the landscape with dry patches of grass, the occasional circling of small purple flowers I used to pluck and tie together in wreaths for my grandfather's head, but what about the way the porches wrap and snap until they connect in one looping square, and their surfaces are coated in all the toads and frogs from the swamp down the street, the bog in the backyard, did you know I'm keeping my heart safe for you, if you don't mind the hauntings then we can head out together, traverse the floors of the ancient and many-floored house with its beautiful rouge carpets, the mermaids stamped into the foyer, the way the kitchen has a habit of grow-ing waxy plastic leaves in coils and its shadow, a sec-ond smaller kitchen, is covered in boughs of ivy and empty pots and pans, beneath lives twisting floors like too-soft bricks, no one knows where to put their cigarette ashes, I want you to take the glasses gently from my face and know their designated spot on the nightstand my heart wants, ragged with haunt, and while you're at it could you watch my back as we descend, I think if I reached for your hand I would twist turn to ash in an instant. And inside these walls which contain the history of the house itself a thousand endless movements crushed in liminal spaces where ghost lobsters and demon crabs glow unnatural shades of amber and azure there is a pasture of velvet, there is a ladder, we ascend between thin layers of kitchens, stacked as one boiling cake on top of another and I'm desperate to make it out of the maze alive—with you by my side—and if you don't mind the way I scratch at my chest when I can't breathe, if you, too, cover all the surfaces during a storm, if you house ruined horses, if you have soft stars in jars atop your highest cabinets, and might you also have a beehive with a pool of honey where the bugs can swim, and did you know there is another four-letter word for love but it hasn't been revealed yet, but would you guess I have something else written on my tongue for you, and could you put away your teeth to listen, but would you take care to not insult the ghosts who have never left this place, so I guess we arrive together, intertwined like strands or rope or hands, we could make it through, you and I, and if we live to see oceans together, would you know to lead me along where it hurts? Would you trust the best shells are a little further out, leave your broken shards in the expertly labeled foyer drawers, then maybe we can make it through just fine, maybe we'll drive like darling flames to lick the salt into soup bowls and stationary holders, well did you know there is a demon holding the core of this home and every time she hears me laugh she shakes, it only serves to bump us closer together, my teeth accidentally brushing your earlobe, I'm going to break your heart if that's okay, I'm going to stoke your crush into a bonfire.

What if we were just two horses in a river?

And we didn't need coral-coded kitchenware, and we weren't good at cooking. Maybe I'm not talking about horses, maybe I'm talking about angels and you're not paying attention, you don't know the difference between cloudy grey hooves and creamy blue wings, you have no self-control, glancing at my hands as they move when I talk, listen I am trying to tell you something important, that last night at the bar when we accidentally stumbled into the backroom, sure I was fingers and fists, your legs were brushing against mine, your eyes were blue then bronze beneath strange strobe lights, there were angels drinking in the fountain and the DJ was playing songs about magic and fury, but what happened when you left me alone against the back wall? You turned to look at me like you've never touched my body, and soon we were rushing the highway back home, our taillights were gold feathers, you told me you didn't know what I wanted out of this life anymore. It's not my fault I'm restless, I want to be taken seriously, I want to own up to a halo, I want a wing bone to stab me so deeply in the heart I turn blue and cold as a stone. So, this is how it goes—you accuse me of lying, after we fought hellhounds in silence, you took the words from the walls, you bowed to the old gods and told me it was just another Saturday night, you don't believe my arguments, you hate the web of forms, you once tried to drown me in lilac foam. Out front, I see birds picking fights with each other's chests, the sky is crunched up against the trees, why can't I stop loving you? Maybe this time, when I need a miracle, I'll sacrifice more than a gauzy evening, I'll take the hands and backs of the young gods, we'll level out my heart, we'll un-carve this wood, I'll stop changing my language to meet your gaze, I'll fade away into the mess halls where Heaven and three separate Hells collide, there is a fourth sphere whose name I don't know, I try to access the space, not warm nor holy, not cold and devoid of fire, there are forty words for Harmony, ninety for Hallowed, none for hate or health, there are no hearts here, I press flowers into my eyes trying to get away from you but your fingers intertwine with an angel and I have to admit I hate how their many blue eyes reflect yours, hate their glittering pentalpha, no longer halo but weapon, they take your cheekbones in their many-fingered hands—those cheekbones I once wrote the worst sonnets of my life over—and then the evening is dips and candles, a dashboard of emotions, you're both growing extra teeth and I'm still here, at the edge of the world, in the mood to be eaten by wolves or water, whichever comes first, you disappear into the backroom, I dissolve into a leach.

Relapse

Gently. Soap your body with your hands. Consider letting your hair grow. Consider making soup for yourself. Be gentle with the towel. Glance in the mirror at the scars and don't think about the men downtown, pool tables and pool water, kissing in the hot tub. You try to take steps away from your body and remain the same. This was supposed to be a fresh start, but you cried at dinner everyone knows you—wound. You are in complete need of help. Want to be soft. Want to feel warm April air on your bare skin and not think of hiding. Blue cotton pants the color of the sky. *Sueños* and clouds and eating without fear. *Sal, si puedes.* But remember the dim booth and soft coral-hued flowers, heart in your teeth? You're lying again, you want there to have been fisherman's stew and tablecloths, everyone knows you were in fact greasy-fingered and shy. Was it noticeable? You're dipping into daydreams. The boys of your past are not the men you know, now. Someone has left a little toy car on the hostess desk. You are no longer gentle in the bathroom but a tired, wishing thing in the restaurant. Want to be a small piece of metal with wheels. *Quiero comunicar con mi madre* about what happened. This isn't about kindness but exhaustion. Wear the wristband and tell yourself this is the last time. Scoop petroleum jelly with your fingers, think about eating it. You've got to be so careful, gentle, careful. You've got to force yourself to be so soft.

Tell me you want to know, and we'll go from there

Hazy days. Everywhere green, muggy, vegetable fields encircled by pines, reminds me of the times we walked near fields of wheat, monarch butterflies, still loved each other, didn't mind highway overpasses, strangers on bicycles, a stray grey cat wrapping its body around legs, the times I went to parties and couldn't enter unless I took all my clothes off. The house with the sharks, the chef with sun tattoos on both his knees, she came with me back then, we couldn't be together, we belonged to the men, so many of us clustered around each other at the edge of the jellybean pool. Bitter, couldn't swim in the expensive water, outcast, eating too many empanadas by the stove, never learned to sew but quick with a needle and skin, railroad tracks, cat claws, praying in the bathroom for breath to return to my lungs. Wonder what you'd do if you knew. Isn't this always how it goes? Warm bar, beer is average, I want them to love me but realize loving means knowing, and knowing is distrust, times I sold tech and gold, have so many rivals I can't go home without hiding, could only pay waitresses in pennies and nickels until work picked up, do you want to know about the times I ran out of clothes, stole from cheerleaders, pocketed statues of blue cows and ice-clear birds, roses blown from glass,

a necklace passed down from many grandmothers,
learned to read stamps on silver? First I'll need you
to adore me, then we can talk about the blood.

Night Tide

Because it was cold in the surf and you went off on that dead shark, pissed about the morning when we tossed confetti like rocks, you had grass in your socks and you told me about the field in all its viridescent moodiness, was going to save your life. You didn't even ask if I could save your life. I have this problem where I think if I just try a little harder, I can do it. I can protect you the way you need me to. I don't know what that way is yet, but do you remember the day we bent like the oak trees and you had a salt cube under your tongue for the dizziness, and we were mimicking the way branches sometimes move in that way where you think to yourself, I'm not alone in this forest, all the ghosts of my past are here too, and each time they catch me starting to doubt they start shaking acorns loose and those are the days we sit at the table and we say what happened to us, without saying *that stuff*, we can name things like loss or ache or exhaustion. Half asleep on the patio out back and you bring me a blanket, but you won't ask how I am doing. When you go back inside, I cry. Anyways, I've been meaning to ask if you're going to bring the shells home with you. I watch as you near the coves, slick grey rocks working as shelter for lobsters and sea glass, you dip your hand in the pool even though it's February and snowflakes freeze in spores on the surface. I want something to remember you by. I want you to give more than you have, or maybe more than you can. Sometimes I wake in the middle of the night, and you're gone, and I think to myself, you're out there, preferring to tell secrets to jellyfish all lilac and dead on the shore.

3. Ghost

I will be wonderful tomorrow

In the dream you return, and we argue in the tomato patches. All I do is try to decipher my own heart. I don't think I'm beautiful when I'm not lying, but he tells me he only enjoys my sentences that are full of hives, needles, pin pricks, he has no idea what I've accomplished with a paring knife, what I could accomplish with a pan. Smack dab in the middle of gauze-infused August, is it my metaphor which is the lie, or my perception of my own reality—that is to say, this daydream which belongs only to me? Maybe I should stop calling everything waxy, green-hued, beautiful, intentional. I don't think your way of looking at the world is honest, it sounds unfocused and sometimes, cruel. I could mimic you, if you wanted. You know what I mean? I could have woken up and told you I had a dream about someone who left, we fought, I considered crying in the dream, I reconsidered crying when I woke up. The coffee was cold but still good, I couldn't stop eating cream cheese. I half-considered writing poetry before work, then remembered I don't know where poems are supposed to end, it's always this tightrope dance of almost-hits and then I lose my edge, I misstep and fall—and whatever it is I'm saying begins to fall apart. That's usually when you point at the

sharp and tell me, there's where the heart lies. What
I want to know is, how do you even know I have a
heart? How do you know I'm even telling the truth,
now? What if I woke up happy, what if instead I
had champagne cheddar? I guess it's your turn to be
forced into trusting me. I guess this is the end—but
it doesn't feel like it. I could keep going. I could keep
lying to you. Did you know if you leave cheese out
long enough, it grows not mold, but wings? Who am
I? And anyway, what good is a poem you can't eat?

Manhattan in January /
And my heart was the
evening

The city has stitches of our souls across town, su-
perimposed beneath blue Saturdays and bug bodies,
the green Christmas lights hanging from the bodega
you love so much, the glow of a raw violet immor-
telle beneath clear plastic awnings, I hang around al-
ley corners in the hopes that I'll see you. But you're
always one step ahead of me, like the light before
it shatters, the train before it stops, a tree bending
before its leaves snap off in a storm, the vault await-
ing a banker's hands, the cocoa, the pretzel salt, the
pigeons, frosted and pear-hued Central Park at four
in the morning, you're rocks and holes in socks and
key-scratched train windows, a third of my veins,
why don't we find out how soft gold is? Why don't
you know how to fix the neon lights and the cos-
tume seams? Even the apartment bursts in edges at
the thought of you, smoke-and-wine-stained you.
When you're back, we lose our money in bars and
the leather seats of taxis, my makeup is blue then all
over my cheeks, you're crying over someone else at
the diner and I'm laughing so hard into my bowl of
cereal that the bartender threatens to kick me out. In
a public cube where sidewalks are full of dazzle and

gum, you kneel and tie my converse at my favorite
intersection, the one with all the plants in the center
and the spray-painted ice cream cones along raised
medians. I miss flights for you, I get lost in book-
stores and I pick up shifts, hoping to see you near
Gristedes, I hear my grandmother's fading language
in my head, I wish you were around back then, to
witness the quiet way she folded money into envelopes from the local bank, gently tugging out singles
for lottery tickets whose numbers were our birth-
days, we could have loved her together, we could
have seen the 99-cent store cat, shabby-grey rat-eater,
you'd have known to save me the holographic journals, you'd have kept the best Pokémon cards for me.
And now we're stamping through Manhattan snow,
I want to tell you about the time I almost tripped
into a lake before grabbing the hand in front of me
but I know you'd care more about whose kisses went
into what poems, you'd rather flirt with me when
I have sprinkles on my eyelashes and a head full of
lust, you're interested in the sewers of my heart but
you won't stay the night, already you're gone before
the pigeons leave the awnings, twist of Tanqueray
between fingers, a flirt with the grill girl before the
rinse of dawn, later you'll duck into bed with a raver
dressed as a fawn and I'll catch the tail-end of your
dalliance, a glint of your star earring before you enter
a cab, you turn around to inspect the block and all

you see is a body hunched over the begonias, gathering flowers for a birthday or a funeral, maybe a wedding, maybe it's better this way. I'm a stranger in your eyes and you're the Brooklyn carousel, coated with rain, glittering gold as a jewel or a life, could you come over this time? It's not that I'm falling for you, I just need someone to keep me honest before the streetlights turn on.

W.

The field around was amber, half-dead; that was just what happened in-between fall and winter. The girls volunteer in their spotted dresses and lion hats, jubilant beneath a grin of moon. It was November, of course it was, sitting on a stool as drunk teenagers tried, and failed, to hit my outline with knives. We'd been broken up for three months. Little else matters. No goodbye in the frosting of a cake, can't leave this town, no more getting lost in the forest in the green-gold dawn. There are rumors of sticky diner counter kisses, waitresses and cooks, her face a toothy grin, her shadow growing like leaves and flowers. Oh, this old thing? A situation, a goose for dinner, you know all about the shiny side of the knife. These days it's funny to care. Northeaster, elsanta, jewels then earliglows, everything is soft, someone's teeth click together, sometimes I wish I were a sheep inside of a wolf. Inside his stomach, I imagine softness. Little places in the rib cage where I could hang my coat. Do wolves wear coats, bear ribs? We'd be unrecognizable in all that weather, scruff, singing then growling, I used to think you would come back. They barely miss my head. Bonnets and reapers, tabasco in bundles of cloth, you were never in love, first act, sweet and singing serrano. I return to the grey light of dawn.

I struggle to get the knives out of the wall. Have I always been this angry? All that lasting impression, always figured you hated my freckles and floppy hair, wanted to keep me stuffed in a box, bluecrop then blueray, lowbush, rabbiteye as you gather misty blue-golds in your little green apron.

Melt

You try not to look at her but you can't help it, the magnetic pull of the evening too much for you to withstand, everyone melting from the first heat of winter, air vents blowing particles around the living room like bits of snow, there is wine and there is laughter, there is alcohol in lime green bottles and appetizers glazed with sugar, a dash of salt, you are on the couch furthest from me, I can't tell if your boredom leads you to desire, to devour, or if this is another party trick, know you put on such a cute personality for the others, this won't end well so I pretend to be her, imagine what it would feel like to glow from within, to wear boots to dinner with ripped jeans, a crushed pack of cigarettes, I excuse myself to the bathroom so I can make faces in the gilded mirror, the wallpaper behind me is full of purple parrots, I get lost on the way back, I am greedy, would turn into your favorite dessert if you asked kind enough, instead we avoid each other, you know too damn well these days I'm a warning bell, you're a gem, you prefer dimly lit hallways of dust and fire, you only love when someone is covered in distress, so I distract myself with the blood-red rocks glasses and soft-billed pelicans stamped on the ceiling in the dining room, heron feathers made of glass dangle from the chandelier, no one can figure out if I twist my stories or my heart into lies, someone asks if I'm going to write about the evening and I respond by eating all the ice in the freezer, later you'll ask if I'll sit next to you and I'll try, really, to pretend I don't have a soul, a body, no blood in my veins, I am a ghost spore, you might trap me in a jar.

We are connected

Like a knot and a restless hand, petals ripped from the stem and the ground which hosts the roots, potato peels and tomato slices for the stew, those days you woke early to your father cooking on the stove and even though you'd fought the night before you knew he would still feed you something made with love, the fact that I have an emptiness inside of me which has a shape and a sound and a face similar to yours, the cavities we have filled with gold foil, the days we went to the lake house and joked about drowning each other so we could come back as silly ghosts in blue robes, the argument and the rain which coated the car, the times I told you I cared and you didn't respond—which is to say, the words and the silence, like birds and rough dogs, halls lined with soot and the small yellow glowing thing which nettles the mind, the times I heard you howling at the moon and asked if you wanted to come inside for a glass of milk, alcohol and a tongue, the gaze and the indifference, static electricity between our clothing and the others in the room, the time I alluded to the blood and you didn't ask further questions, similar to the bandage and its carrying case, though I would never be so bold to assume you're cotton or needle, you are restless, you're on my mind, sundresses in the summer, say yes to the kitchen patterns, say no to the wrong pair of wings, say you'll survive dinner, thanks for trying to stop the decay, it will happen again.

What to do

With the empty heart at the party, who would have
thought things would be any different, devouring
unnameable drinks in the foyer, golden peach lamps
and flaking foil, pieces of fruit peel curling into letters, reminding me of your name, reminding me of the
open-mouthed way I wish I could say love or devour,
instead I'm sorry, I've eaten what was left of my hu-
manity, I still have a story about pleading but I don't
think you want to hear it, I have dozens of ghosts
trailing behind me like damaged dresses, yellow hat
and alone in the diner, sometimes you seem like your
heart has valves and other days you're an empty case,
hard outer shell of a candy, flying saucer full of rainbow gems, bad for my teeth but I'm dreaming about
you anyway, sorry I was close enough to put my head
in your lap, sorry I didn't leave first, I never expected the moon to rot away in the sky, never expected
the hands and have you had enough of me yet, do
you know I can never go back, do you know what it
means to be driving in a car with someone you're not
in love with, encased in rain, someone's hands are on
the steering wheel, you don't recognize this feeling
of safety, but it's safety, little messy heart with a hook
in the center, of course the whole point is to smoke
too much, to ask you to help with the shaking hands,

rough terrain, this is another way I'm dressing up what really happened, which is to say my body is the temperature of frazil crystals and I build little homes around my memories to keep myself warm.

I am running out of ways to say

Oh my god / couldn't stop the river if I tried / the times we held smooth pebbles in our hands / and I knew nothing of mud or tire tracks / my heart wants to take things too far / don't want to talk about / bleeding / how do I explain this feeling / your laughter on ghost-smoke mornings / how I want to show you the iron masks / the times I wanted to kill my / freshwater crabs in small green buckets / the way my collarbone is a magnet against yours / long night / green jars / everyone is cute / the room is old-gold like an oyster / you talk about money / like it / means nothing / I can't stand too close / my breathing a loose / horse / hooves in the backyard / prints in the sand pit / the time of the bandages / sorry I was sore / sorry about sour / saw my blood / it reminded my body / of loss / of god / how I wanted to run / into your arms / when you told me you / understood wounds / and feelings / this is nightmare week / this is the year after the year I quit that shit / the day after the night of blood / do you want to know or should we crush / the ice for the drinks / I'll bring sugar I'll / bring excuses for heat / in my face / my teeth / hold back the hurting hand / from your healing gaze / it's not about screaming / ghosts woven into sheets / caramel buds / soft night / everyone is kind / should

I stop wanting to / dive / into late winter water / the road leading to missing / I'd have to tell you everything / and oh how / you'd regret me / but we could be / magical four / in the morning / water glass / doves up sleeves / a feeling that is more banshee / than boy / don't want to give away sad / gums of stars / would have loved to see you tip / top-shelf liquor / brine from the Atlantic / those days you reminded me sunlight existed / but the bleeding / this feeling / of dreaming / nights I woke up screaming / will you hold me or / haunt me.

Guilty August

Summer house, seashells, the mothers gather in their circle, discuss what to do with the daughters, but why talk on the haziest day of August, they wonder about fuss and whether the daughters left the house wearing shoes, some of the mothers are very hungry, some are making little cuts through the air, their hands like knives, they are slicing invisible ribeye steaks for the daughters who have all gone down to the river to play a game called who-gets-to-drown-today, they are reading stories about daughters, tightly bonded, white-knuckling their summers until school starts again and all the sons return from the shore, the sons who barely know the difference between crabs and lobsters, couldn't tell you a claw from an acorn an ache from the empty stomach of a gutted tree, no matter the sons are gone today and the fathers were never there to begin with. Everything is sweet and green, everything is daughters, the mothers can be heard laughing over hills and their laughter forms a bond between the offspring they decide no one will drown today, they lay their bodies in the river, there are no wolves to eat them, no sharp hooves their dresses inflate with water, their lighters float downstream everything is a dream, they promise to forgive each other they make small crowns out of river rocks, laugh about how the water isn't salty, nothing like the water for sons and fathers, the sea full of scales and household items and the promise of death, the daughters are making water angels, though they will never become holy or strong or rare enough.

**I can't find you by the shore anymore, but I
pretend you're still here /
We make dinner for our children**

There are fish and daughters, salt and a regretful sea,
unfair the wildlife doesn't care about me and what
do you want to do about dinner, should we tell the
daughters to give up their sea bass and perch, should
we sun the fish or place them in shady buckets, is your
favorite color still blue, do you know of alligator in
the fields, their mouths opened for rain, you were
smoking in the back door, ignoring me, obsessing
again over the harbor, she's not coming back, left you
with me and them, I've also said goodbye to my husband could be your partner or cluster, if you wanted,
a fry or broken-down car, the ring on your finger,
thick as jam jars within which we once placed fins,
starved starfish found crusty on the shore, jam jars
with milk and small minnows with small mouths,
white peaches and ombre peaches, you don't want
me to help you anymore, you want the daughters
to tie your hair with tendons, I see your body most
nights, out with lanterns looking for your wife, likely
eaten by the sea, wish I could keep you company but
these days I barely keep my mind local, I am a freshwater chicken, I am a terrible catch, I channel rivers into static, pretend I'm sleeping when you, soft-

footed, drape a blanket over my body, this couch is lonely, our love will never be in season, but the next morning you wake like nothing happened, hair still with half-broken blood, asking me if I'll help grab tomato buckets, open clams, make her stew.

During which I make up a series of lies for you in August

For example, it's the end of July and the moon is in my backyard again. I turn into a very small bird and haunt you. I am a rotten peach and a worm-filled jam jar. I didn't eat the last of your jelly seeds and even though you told me you wouldn't leave the windows tossed open during a storm, your ex's perfume lingering in the foyer, told me you'd stop smoking yet draped over the walls are small silver ghosts, even after the argument in the berries—patchwork of pink-red-blood from crow beaks, half-eaten smeared raspberries and those little red berries which are poisonous but whose name I forgot, yes—even after all that, I am not a person. I am a drama, I am your Sunday, sand below lightning, wave that makes you hate the sea, darling but not yours, don't love you. Could let go any time. Want to turn the cheese into moons, water into limes, did you know I used to be a monster? I begin to wonder how long confessions go on before the priest gets tired and walks away.

Corallium

1.

You're telling her jokes as you walk through shallow water, star grass and white plants with yellow centers floating amongst potato chip bags as bright and rainbow as dying stars, you keep missing red soda caps among too-red algae, you are so tightly wrapped around leaving me that you don't notice I'm still trailing behind.

2.

Breakfast near the marsh beds, the ocean twills, surf is clear for now, but tomorrow we'll rise again, early with trash bags to clear discarded items from surfers and parties, do you remember the time you found old flower necklaces wrapped around fish necks, do you still love wearing lip-gloss the color of coral reef, it's these early mornings when the house is still filled with life and we're drinking coffee and I think to myself, you might still love me, but I'll never ask. Late nights we sit on the porch eating burnt strawberry cake, puffy pastry twists, I hate the raspberry-hued stomachs of crabs, I hate the sharks feeding by the steps who act like no one can see their appetite, but danger is near and your newest crush forgot her anklet by the shore.

3.

Disassociating by the sink, wondering if you still take your eggs the same way, do you know all the words for sugar, can you feel the memory of my jellyfish sting beneath your fingertips, still the burn, still my mind tosses itself back to the surf, I used to cast spells with the sand, wrote your name in the high tide line and the sand crabs knew I was losing track of myself they didn't care, I'm not sure I even do, now. The surf arrives and disappears every day at the same time. The ocean tries again to heal itself, tossing bleached reef skeletons to my feet, the shoal reminds me of your hair, I'm forgetting what color your eyes are, I'm forgetting my own name. Do I know me, anymore?

4.

March stacks frost on top of the roof. Clear blue of the sky, the birds have disappeared, we remain with mouths and hands and huckleberry galettes, there are so many people on this earth I could care for, yet I only ever want you. I don't know that I care when she asks to borrow my eyeliner. Says, we don't need to take care of the beach today, everyone is going for walks on the ice paths, would I like to come along? She offers me her gloves and scarf, ignores the heat in my face, what do I want, will there be owls, will one of you catch me if I slip, linger by the mangroves and I've brought wishes in my pockets, but I won't let them out until it's time.

5.

Soon: rain. Ice, full of broken shell pieces, a twenty-
five-cent rubber ball from the supermarket down the
street, a droplet of blood from when I woke too early,
found the two of you quiet in the kitchen booth and
walked the path alone, don't worry, I've always been
good at this part.

6.

When I was a child, I thought parrot fish could sing.
I preserved sand dollars like they were pale, hot coins.
I drowned my feelings in the cove, but they came
back in lobster boxes, coated in iron and rusted root
knots, the sea wants nothing of my dreams, I rose
like a tornado or a woman and prayed to catsharks,
took my past to the drain, you said I couldn't write
an honest sentence for the life of me, well how about
I try? I am tripping gently on the back paths as the
others slide forward, they are singing and dreaming and wearing coats and I don't know how to say
goodbye, I grab onto my life with claws and bites,
I've even started saving the trash from the surf, what
was somebody thinking tossing their shoe into the
waves?

7.

I will be honest from now on. I will find you in early kitchen light, screw another frost walk, and we can talk. I'll show you where I've drawn the lines, say, look, here's where I was a parasite, I tied grass into knots and locked myself out of my own heart. This isn't honest enough yet. Do you still want to sit near me during storms?

8.

I have feelings for you that don't warrant their own poems. Soon she arrives, silt nails, and charms you away.

Sugar Tide

The heart is coated in ribbons and bells, I guess this
was always how things would go, crouched in the
sandcastle made of hands, you in your mother's faded Cape Cod sweatshirt and me in your pants, this
feeling is an error, half of the day is swallowed by caverns, I have to reteach my hand to draw rabbits, L.
you are here with your map and glitter nails, this way
out of the sea town, it's even worse than I thought,
you laugh at my jokes and my stomach turns into a
soft pink snow-cone house, the smoke alarm in the
kitchen is going off again and the mothers are all
cackling, we can hear them over the incoming waves,
they don't know how to turn it off so they shatter the
plastic with a hammer, things are hysterical, the sea
is ribeye-red and the seals hang out before low tide,
damn if this isn't risk, a hazard, a hoping ache to see
the sharks together, what do you call euphoria you
can't share, why are you in all my diaries, you're air-
drying your hair on a rock and I'm trying to think
of a clever way to entertain you, like what if my nail
beds had forks, is it hard to tuck mice into match-
box beds, do you want jolly rancher eggs, should we
talk about what happened? No, let's hide my look in
a hole, we will bury the memory and when they excavate my mind there will be Mary statues, an octo-

pus wall, a very bored looking girl selling buckets of candy, answer my riddles three, my father's forehead is visible just beyond the rock face, you hate to find a way out, you want to see more of my mother but she becomes a pink hair dryer screaming a name I can't stop thinking about, little lilacs on my grandfather's head, talk all that talk but don't leave the beach, later the mothers will tell us stories over dinner, we'll take photos in the ivy, I'm trying not to become hysterical but the urge to grab your arm and talk about the atrium, and oh god your mother is witnessing me, let's make no promises, let's dance into kernels of sand.

Coyote

Everyone tells me it's the year for a stigmata. I text my
friend who says *if they knew, they wouldn't be making this joke.* I never touched my feet. I don't know
how to speak to you without talking about blood.
Every day I think we're getting closer. Every day I
try to make a survival plan for what happens if you
leave. It's impossible for me to love someone without thinking of goodbyes. We spend all week talking
about how I eat like a coyote, I've told three people
now about the eating disorder, I wish I could forget.
We joke about how I'm constantly eating scraps. I
joke about how I'm constantly writing about blood.
Some kind of twisted little wolf, coyote but half my
body is eaten by rot, underneath the streetlamps I
am changing into a mutt, there is invisibility, there is
this startling ribbon of bandage, the promise of June,
will you stick around during the hot months, I don't
want a seam, I never learned how to scream. Evening in the room, lamp like a sun, today is enough,
will tomorrow suffice? Cheese, crackers, chocolate,
one bite of chicken, mostly rice, too much caffeine,
I have not changed, six cucumber disks, two pieces
of bread rolled into balls, bacon slice, lick clean the
knife, will you get sick of the afternoon? Three chocolate covered almonds, mostly water, I dream I am

someone who has excellent taste in beer, I dream I am excellent at human connection, I can endure the heat of love and not instantly think about harm, my disposition is an everlasting gobstopper, my character is a gummy worm, my arms are marble, overripe tomatoes, unfeeling, last of the season. When you're not looking, I am a glass of champagne, I am tucking myself into the cabinet while our friends toast the end of the semester. I sit among your plates and cups, think about loss. I think about green grapes. Bet you didn't know coyotes can't get keloids. Bet you didn't know my doctor still thinks my arms are so soft.

I keep following you home /
Maybe this time we'll be beautiful

1.

We're alone, the lambs and the dogs have gone into lilac pastures where sticky circles and dried mud lay undisrupted, your house feels hundreds of miles away and each time I look back I see it deflating until your dishes and kitchens and bedside tables are nothing more than a puffy glowing thing in the grass.

2.

Next to me, you're making bold claims about love, sweeping the air with your hands, trying to conjure the woman of your dreams out of the last dewdrops of June-dawn, I told the others I'd never trust you again yet we're out here, combing animal hair out of our clothes at night, asking one another if we'd like more milk heated on the stove, pouring coffee, shaving pale cheese into a bowl, digging viridescent rose peaches out of their hiding places in the back garden.

3.

Your eyes, normally almond, turn bright in the setting sun. Soon it will be dark, soon there will be dogs with jaws and their soft friends come to lead us back to the house, I don't have the strength to tell you I

want to stay right here, I want to live on this patch
of weeds until my heart falls apart and I begin a final
unraveling. It wasn't automatic. We walked horses
across streams and I hated your boots, your hands,
the holes in your jeans, I went to bed frustrated by
simple human gestures which haunted me, woke up
twisted in sheets and your bird got into my room
again, now the animals are singing at four in the
morning, the moon has disappeared, I hear you slow
walk out of your room, knocking on her door so you
can feed the chickens together from slightly rusted
pails.

4.

I know there's a way out of this space yet I want to
stay lost, I hate when you tell me to stop resisting
softness, I don't believe you, don't believe there is an
ending, I'm going to follow you back inside and anyway, whoever knows what's going on, who else have
you invited to witness your hungry thunder longing,
there are so many of us sitting, sleeping, talking in
the field, I don't know why I wake up every day and
crawl back to you, I'll leave and you won't come with
me, if I were to walk straight into the setting sun you
wouldn't come with begs and tears, you resist the
paths I walk, I'm getting so sick of this but I can't
give up.

5.

Later, we eat dinner outside. Everyone laughs at your jokes; you take turns twisting the knife into a roast still coated in cooking strings. She told you she wanted you back and now we have to suffer through dinner-as-theatre, dinner-as-excuse, dinner full of claws and fog, the red of the shed, I want someone to take me out back and place me soft by the half-broken horse ring, this isn't about heels or hearts or literally trust, I woke up crying again and baby I want the pine trees with their permanent leaves, I want navy-blue shivers, I wouldn't mind coffee grinds in a chipped mug, I want reasons to take my heart to the waiting, jawed things, I could toss the pulpy lattice off, play it cool like I have an apple or a bundle of sweaty blueberries stuck together in a drama, next thing you know the creatures are biting at my tendons and I'm disappearing before night, before longing, before velvet green grass regrows next spring.

6.

Again, I stay. I say yes when someone asks to feed me a spoonful of something hot and delicious. We keep smiling at each other, I can hear my grandmother asking me if I know the difference between gratitude and *gañir, gimotear* and geraniums in her hair, I accidentally push my wine glass onto the bricks, and no one cares but you. In the kitchen, you kiss Cabernet

Sauvignon off my thighs and the others wave to me, I pretend I'm washing a hand in the sink, covering my mouth with my fingers, I fake-laugh and you take my heart all the way out of its case.

Evergreen

Hood of the car, letters written in chalk, late-day sand, the times you hid in the closet during arguments, wrapped fabrics around your body, tried to create wings but couldn't fly, always stopping before window's lift, dreaming lately of goldfinches and cardinals, sometimes starlings, always blackbirds and downy woodpeckers, the suitcase of the exorcist is secretly packed with red maple leaves, in another life the possession leads to tulip poplars and sugar maples, no one is stacking chairs upside-down, everything is oak and gum, there are mothers who banish ghosts before they enter the premises, planting walnuts, sculpting rivers, allowing for dogs, make room for sourwood and sour daughters, hickory, cedar, umbrella pine, you dream about him. Empty heart like a hood or a wing, there will come a time to discuss the blame and the fix, butterflies and Joe Pye, the ghost pipes keep you up at night, you are root and bread, trout, bell, full of pink fire, he sits in the garden and watches you dance in the evening, there is no mercy, this is a story older than women or witches, this has been a long time coming, how long, how come, things aren't fair, *fontanesiana* is a moist mountain, rubbery-blue, the net grasps the foliage, the *silene virginica* is the color of the sky, you want to touch his throat, for him to catch you as you trip over the slope, grey flower, you are fungus, poison, a neighboring spy stem, the culprit and the thief, add too: the mugged house and the stove emptied of all coils, your tracks are gone but the whiskey fungus remains, even though your crush is evident as turkey tail, stacked pattern of desire, wrote your secrets on crowded parchment, peeled pears from your shoulders, even after you survived, he might not want to know about the blood, violet teeth, oyster bites, honey from the ocean, you talk too much, this could be good, this could be May, lemon butter and bird bridges, when is the right time to tell him this forest mix is a lie, you are not a human anymore, just a flat lantern with a corroded soul.

1.

It was dawn, the trees turned gold, each branch slicked in old cold berries, each leaf as sweet-smelling as a newly sliced orange and I was living my life again as if we were the same person in the same body. To the left of the forest wall were bursts of honeysuckle, a grey bird in a nest, someone else's heart twisted into a crown, I asked if you were dreaming and you laughed in that gentle way of yours, said *we aren't anything,* and it didn't hurt as much as when the arrow pierced my flesh. Here I am, you, I am gold, I am pain and summertime, a fracture, your favorite hooked fish, your vision, your eclipse, a baby wolf not yet understanding the responsibility of having a jaw.

2.

Try as I might to pause the gap, it widens. We fall in. The earth whispers, *que bella,* she's talking about you not me and *la luna* begs me to surrender, destroy *mis dientes,* everything becomes apples, onion marmalade, a bundle of goats, brie and honey, a hole fit for a comb, a fang dipped in Manchego.

3.

Gold space, plants and hate, broken record player, hands *tirando mi corazón* off the balcony, a bend and twirl then you're all satin and still in the loveseat, the others *arrastrándome* and we head to the dining room where one by one you will consume my life energy until there is nothing else. It's like, why not me, couldn't you have taught me to stitch my seams back together? We could have saved the city and taken on your exes head first, instead you make me into a poltergeist and I pull the Hudson from its resting place like a cape or the mouth of a shell, I open the water and send it to consume the apartment, *quiero hablar contigo,* let's melt the eulogies into glittering buckets, there is no noise when I come for your history, blue lamps then white, the wrong alphabet but it doesn't matter, there's a fire in the medicine cabinet, there is our sister braiding your hair in the bathroom mirror, you don't care I'm gone, you are eating hazelnuts by the stove and no one seems to mind when I drape my rains all over the room.

4.

You know, once I told you a story about a mother who locked her daughter in the refrigerator room and made her eat away at frost and lovely, cold, blue things, sadness neatly tucked into a pastry, she couldn't find the hallway out, she drowned in doors and drawers, ripped out the rug with her teeth, *yo sé que tú no es yo, pero verano* comes anyway, slick with beetles and grandmother's emeralds, let's say goodbye to each other, let's tell stories the way they're meant to be told, spoken, coin clicks, perfume bubbles, roses inside my chest, let's complicate things.

5.

My heart, independent of me, dependent on you. Come late, come dawn, come over, come back, come and doodle mushrooms on my shoulder, come what may, come hell, come blood and ships and ropes and sea, come salt and eyes and freckles and hair, *ven tarde, ven ahora mismo, come oro, come* flower fields and falling apart on the floor, come with ripe knuckles and bruises, my hickory, my throat, come grief, come alive or as a ghost—it doesn't matter—falling apart or flying, a failure or a walk in the evening, a fire, a weed, my father or yours, an accompaniment and a dream, at once I am asleep and then you're here breathing in my ear, next time I'll call you by all your names, next time will be different, delicate, serene, a list fit for the kingdom of summer, everything will be steeped in rusty *verano* and nothing will hurt.

6.

Abre la puerta for the flowers, the procession of mourners, the moon, the priest who carries her hip bones, they are bringing bags of my hurts and amongst the pain are button mushrooms, cups, enoki and oyster, a portabella large enough to house a horse or a heart, a family seated at the breakfast table floats through the window like a dream or a stream, everything is egg yolk and my mother takes my history to the kitchen table, she rolls my arms into pines, she dresses me with king oysters, my body has been consumed a thousand times and it will be consumed a thousand times more, dried porcini, hedgehogs and lion's mane, cremini and truffle, this isn't about the time they brought me to the forest of death but it could be, over dinner you accuse me of not healing enough to take care of another person let alone myself, you tell me if I don't start putting my body back together then I'm going to ruin everything, but what do you know? Is my body not already together, ribbed, lobster, chili, maroon, a ruby, a company of wounds?

7.

The walls in her room have been painted over dozens of times, you have to hit the doors with your hips, you don't know what I would do to enter a new space, the pigeons are high on the stoop, the pizza place is open twenty-four hours a day and they sell glow-in-the-dark pepperoni and mushrooms, they line plastic dinosaurs on the counter where we deposit money, they tell me I don't have to pay because I'm a ghost but even a ghost has dues. I feel I'm in love, a knife twist, the secret beneath an apple juice lid, pop rocks and punch, I reveal myself to you in carefully curated lists of birds, nuts, satchels, fabrics, tendons, lies.

I wish I had been alone

I leave for the coast at dusk. Half expecting we'll fall apart at the next state line, I pretend I don't see your body looming above mine in the dark of the foyer. When I was younger, I loved this room. There were eggs in baskets, I don't remember if there were fairy lights, I know the wood creaks in some places, the kitchen is still dim and covered in soft tiles, I heard a rumor you once had enough money for a heated floor, whatever happened to that, whatever happened to the vegetables in jars you promised me. But it's past time, I'm lying on a wicker couch, I left my phone in the other room, you opened without the code, reading through my messages in the dimensions of the moon, I wonder if you leaned against the cabinets when you learned I didn't love you, did you hold your face when you read I was scared of you, did you drink the rest of the wine, did you reconsider your fists? But the night was fading, and in the morning, we keep driving.

My car doesn't have air conditioning, but we won't be bothered until we reach Georgia. By then, we'll both be sweating, I'll take the wheel, it's my first time driving for twenty-five hours but it won't be my last time. I don't remember all the places we stop, just know you didn't slap me until I quit school and returned home a month later, I know before we were yelling, your voice was so loud I began to wonder if the others in the hotel heard us, if they did why didn't someone say something, when we went to the pool that next night why didn't they ask if I was okay, you cornered me in the water and asked if we could start over, told me your name and shook my hand like the past six months were a joke. The floor was warm, the air thick with love bugs and I noticed a centipede sleeping beneath a rubbery blue chair. Your father paid for everything, I remember losing money, but I don't remember eating, where did we stop to get water, I know once in the hills of New York State we paused on a cliff, and I told you I was thinking of dropping out of school.

When I arrived to the new apartment, my heart was a cavern, missing stalagmites but not lacking in eyes, I lay awake in a bed coated in flowers and considered the ceiling fan, I considered someone outside chain-smoking cigarettes, I called my ex and begged him to take me out. You and I didn't text those days, I don't remember how you got home, only know you took the next flight out and I had five hundred dollars to my name and no toothbrush. A week later and I'd be down to ninety, I was missing my hairbrush when I left again. This time the sun already set, the palm trees making me nauseous as I drove across five-lane highways, I got lost and crashed my car into a field, I stayed at a motel that only fed its residents pizza and coke.

I return later, to my mother's house. There are crosses above the doorways, she greets me with a pot of rice and tells me never to leave again. I keep track of my history in journals but when asked what happened I can't remember. I erase others' numbers from my phones, I think of emailing her, instead I pretend like nothing happened and try to rewrite my story from scratch. Outside, the backyard has turned tangerine. The porch shakes as I walk across it. I've torn my loves to shreds, I return to the restaurant that evening, borrowing my sibling's clothes and apron, pretending like nothing happened, I pick up a tray of empty glassware and keep my head down until eventually my heart regrows into a fist.

Down narrow halls, black-and white photographs of buildings I've never seen before sway when we brush shoulders, there are hundreds of orchids in the bathroom, everyone shouts in the kitchen, asking me if I want to sit on milk crates out back, do I want mashed potatoes and rice, what am I willing to give up for food, what am I willing to give up for a good tip? Weeks twist into months and I'm a waitress, I

tie my apron too tight, I keep candy in my pockets,
I fawn and dazzle until I make enough money to
get out of there. It starts out slow. The itch of anxiety, my unawareness of trauma, thinking that word
only meant deep cuts from bottle caps on television,
maybe a complicated birth in the backstory of my
mother's life, I thought trauma was the wound on
my aunt's foot we healed with lemon juice, I thought
I was better than stones and stories, but I was in the
back of the house with a knife in one hand, a cold
beer in the other.

This way, guides my manager, his hand heavy on my
bleeding shoulder, he can't tell, my uniform is black
and I wipe any stains out in the sink, I stick my fingers
in the shallow water as others clean the floors, pretend I'm inspecting mollusk shells from our seafood
special, I pretend the pale red floor is the bottom of
a sea, but if that's true why aren't there more crabs,
if we're on land why am I still suffocating? I forget
I'm supposed to follow, I forget how to fold my body
into a cage when yelled at. He'll apologize the next
day, telling me I was right all along but it's too late,
the damage is already crusted. He knows nothing of
scars and metal, he doesn't use knives unless it's for
the salmon, his favorite metal forms a tongue which
inserts itself perfectly into a once-sealed oyster, does
he know these shells are made of layers of calcium,

does he know bones can be beautiful when not tampered with, they grow into rainbows? I wonder if I'll grow wonderful out of the hole in my body, maybe this time I'll be ridged, I'll be sharp, I'll have more arms than I can count, imagine how many drinks I could pour, how many fingers I could use for lessons, I'd be so golden.

I'm still sharp but I'm in the front of the house and everyone's yelling to get inside. The man who owns the clock shop is here, my ex is cleaning menus with Windex, the executive chef eyes me from his perch in the cold window, asking if I want to see a tiny grey crab. Always with the legs and the soft bodies, why don't we want to show each other damage, why does everyone want to know why I left, why doesn't anyone want to know how to save me? I consider, briefly, saving money under my mattress, I consider the education system, I consider the smooth neck of a Heineken. We smoke joints in the parking lot, I don't know if I can save my own life, but I can try. As long as I am a mirror, as long as I am fast, I can outrun their needles, I can outpace this place, and how was I to know come July I would be gone, lost to the wheat fields? There are no trees, something about the farms at night are haunting, but I have his goodbye folded over in my pocket and if it comes down to it, I'll become a ghost if I have to, I'll turn invisible, maybe give up my jaw, I'll do anything to stay away.

Keeping track of February

1.

I've never seen you as happy as you were last night. I want to hold your hand, so you don't slip on lake ice.

2.

Dozens of deer starfish, burnt and concealing a peachy stomach, make me cry. I wonder what it would be like to go home together, I wonder if you could save my life.

3.

The way all fires remind me of the past, when we walked through your family's sculpture forest, and all the iron and wire scared me.

4.

I see the mushroom castle out of the corner of my eye, shrouded in midnight, there are foxes asleep on the front steps and inside is someone who will help me protect my heart. Inside are pots of overflowing soup, there are cold floors and bridges between rooms, there is a room called "Loss Space" where I go at night to grieve, and there is a balcony coated in patches of blue mold and discarded frog toes. All evening, I sit in the kitchen, waiting for you to find me.

5.

You might sit across from me, you might open the
fridge where we keep phantom eggs and queen toast,
frosted butter sculptures, the pitcher of blue snowflake sangria that you love so much.

6.

You might say you love me.

7.

A group of foxes is called *a star*, a cluster of stars is
called *a banquet*, stacks of dishes at a banquet are
called *desires*, there is a bucket under my bed for my
tears but now it is filled with leaves, and at the bottom of the bucket is your necklace, discarded at a
party, I remember I helped you with the clasp, I remember I apologized when I became overwhelmed
by your hair, which smelled like lilacs.

8.

You might sit by me while I bathe, dagger in your lap,
ready to crush any ghost elk that dare disguise them-
selves as men, proclaiming their adoration for me
but you know they want to eat my crush like it's rare
and pepper-coated, you might save me, you might
wonder if I'll ever reveal my true self to you.

9.

Your body fits in the Black Tupelo, which has created a chair for you, but not me, I sit cross-legged
and looking into your clear-ash eyes, you are lifting
your hands in the air and carving a shape, see? I do
see, your magic twists a coastline out of thin air, fingers spark with salt bursts, thorns that are blue and
bluer, palms rain, don't you miss these spaces? You
ask, but I'm too busy gazing at the space between
your thumb and finger to be of much help.

10.

So, I might trust you. Let me try and describe that
feeling—take your shoulders like you do, press your
back against mine, close your eyes to the velvet ivy
and windowless windows, suddenly, I might have
something to say to you.

11.

Your red cape in the water looks a lot like blood.

12.

There is this falling pressure and it tastes like cinnamon sugar.

13.

You raise your hands on a Tuesday; the house opens
its doors, the forest knits together, ivy and assured, as

if I could ever feast with anyone but you, clear eyes are an ice storm, a glass of water tucked away on my nightstand, you tell me to come closer, I do not feel ashamed.

14.

The water is a mirror. We carry bags of seeds into the winter wood, you told me once you thought you could twist a forest in a forest until the green was a tunnel and the sunlight was maybe. I am afraid of the lake, but I go anyway, propping open the lid of the cedar box with my foot as you fetch seeds, excitedly naming primrose, sage, merry bells, but these aren't for the root zone, these are for the valley. I nod, wondering if you'll hold my hand on the way back, lungs still coated in ice shards from the time I slipped and fell from the bank into the mud.

15.

You've left indigo milk caps in my sink. I walk the frost path to thank you but you're not home, and all the candles are dim. I see antlers in the kitchen and wonder.

16.

Unnatural light and fruits you can't eat. You wonder why I am looking at you during dinner. I take desire and hide it in the cabinet. That evening, everyone is

flushed and doubling down in conversation, no one
stops playing music, the kitchen overflows, the sky is
envious.

17.
When you catch me outside, you shrug.

*I guess we should replace the fire so your sister can see
her sheet music.*

I try not to grab your face. Instead, I go home with a
bat whose bed is a green stained-glass box, we could
have an affair but I'm not hungry enough.

18.
Do you want me to tell you, or do you want to go for
a walk?

19.
Shattered, we embrace. What I thought were wings
are now claws. You eat my love and I let you, alight
from within in the place where there could be a heart,
a bundle of teeth in cheese cloth, a prize, a secret, a
candle stick, a clock, a meadow, a person, a sparkle,
a parted mouth, a riddle, a rain on the house, and
a forest in hushed mountains, soon I am twist then
flick, my mouth is gone, I am the pink lightning bolt
which once resided in your chest, but after the spell

I'm free, no body of mine could ever hope to properly convey the rush of heat and bandages, the curve of paws and tear-streaked cheeks, you are melting my stomach, my history escapes through an open window and bursts into a thousand blue-flecked shells with eyes and mouths and good looks.

20.

Mango caramel chocolate in squares. Caramel bacon, blue chocolate ribbon, strips of peppermint bark, ginger bundled in green cloth, I press my face to the glass and contemplate what I want to eat the most. There are snowflakes drizzled in whiskey-infused white chocolate, there are trees made entirely out of sugar, I begin to wonder if the lamps too are crystalline, if the water has been infused with batter, why the air smells so delicious and chilled despite how the heat is blaring through the vents. Outside, it is in the single digits, wind blowing clover around the street, clouds overhead bear the potential for rain, snow, maybe later there will be sleet. I wear your scarf; I walk home alone.

21.

I trip, I eat paprika, I hide in mother's lace folds, nights you disappear, the piano doesn't let me play it, you may never light the path with me but you did hold my hand in the harp room and everyone wondered if the moon was a bad influence or if you were just trying to support me after I winded myself chasing blue mycelia beetles, you're only there to prop me up because I'm prone to falling in lakes, they don't know my love is blue for you.

22.

You hold my heart when we're eating soup.

23.

You carry me through violet fields, my body is draped over your back like a wet butterfly, there is no wind and the only howling you hear is from a sob, I cried and the forest caught my voice, tossing loss from limb-to-green-hand until finally the sound burrows into the earth, its new hiding place among rubber balls, a red shovel, twin antlers, a letter I once wrote begging you to come to my window, what do I do now that the earth has my shame in its mouth?

24.

Why not tell me? It's the last secret either of us has.

25.

Sugar. Finally, Saturn cake. Clementines, beautiful blue beaded lobster, salted tomatoes, maple, rose chips, chiffon, your hips, coco, glass bread, crystal, must we be near the others?

26.

Mars, a Saturn ring, an achievement, a god both still and quiet, a becoming, the day I wrapped love in a piece of uncooked pasta, cold flakes, sweets, bubbles, masses, watching, I want you and I'm not still.

27.

There is frosting in my hair when I wake up, I recall I was up late eating sticky buns, I love baked goods and the cool of the day, eventually I'll swallow the breeze, I want to remain strange, you said I should rest easy, you said there is magic hidden in fire blossoms, perhaps in glue, and when we meet you walk me to the dining hall without holding my hand, I prepare my face, the pre-dawn lights are still on, when you press me into the fridge my heart wakes slowly.

28.

Rivulets. Clean pebbles, chipped glassware, the moths have been enchanted so they hiss. When I don't see you that evening, I take soil in my hands and write a letter explaining that you are my home.

29.

Three minutes shy of midnight you're knocking at my window, face unreadable. I let you inside, wishing longing were not alive, but you're not empty-hand-

ed, you've sewn me a new pair of wings and when
we embrace, I notice you smell of salt, blueberries,
maybe petals. The wind rattles the doors, but you
flick your wrist, calming the month, and we don't
come up for air, not even when the day collapses in
on itself, and we're left locked outside of time, but I
don't mind, I send loss running.

Lago

The daughters windswept in their cotton pants and soft sweatshirts, their mothers bitter and drinking in the daytime, everyone sitting *en la mesa* for a grim discussion: your *abuelito,* gone missing, turned up ghost. Forgive yourself, you were naive when everything went down. Not to admit there was an absence of power. Baby-faced and amongst the June bugs, everything was boring until the storms arrived. She was a crystal in your mind but your mother hated her and so she disappeared into the lake. When you walk home at night, she is dazzling, marsh of bones, crystallized marrow, her muscle is peaks, her eyes are satisfied and everything smells of lavender, vanilla, your mother's hair dye, it's all so complicated, yes, the freckles, yes distrust and distressed jeans, holes in the towels, water falls off the roof in small globes. Your sisters in the bathroom, painting their faces with glitter, smudged eyeshadow, their hair is long, and their nails are sharp. Style is a thing of the past. Grandfather hides beneath the table, blue pajamas and silk night shirt. Been gone a long time, still defiant, he's eating a banana-flavored popsicle, the same kind he bought you at the lake when you were sixteen and didn't have language for her, not even *crush* or *love,* just knew people at school hated you and you cared so much. The mothers stir sangria, its hue akin to a bruise. You have nightmares of fists to your face. *Entonces, la noche.* Goodnight to the loose-limbed horses in the field, the mean girls who swept your friend into a forest and turned her into a witch, your ex's blunt wraps and callouses on your fingers, goodbye to summertime and hello to pain, sure there's jealousy, worrying, a constant alarm pulsating in your mind. *Pero,* what does it matter? *Sólo tu* and your heart's fundamental need for acceptance. Time runs late. Your grandfather hovers over your sisters at the sink, applying fluoride to his teeth.

Author Bio

Sam Moe is the author of *Heart Weeds* (Alien Buddha Press), *Grief Birds* (BS Lit), and *Cicatrizing the Daughters*, forthcoming in Spring 2025 from FlowerSong Press. Her chapbook, *Animal Heart*, won second place in the 3-Day International Chapbook Contest, judged by Diane Seuss. Her fiction, memoir, and poetry has appeared in journals such as Brink Literary, Peatsmoke, Thirty West Publishing, Invisible City, The Texas Review, The Southeast Review, The Penn Review, and others. She has received nine Pushcart nominations and ten Best of the Net nominations. She has attended the Sewanee Writers' conference and received fellowships from the Longleaf Writers' Conference, Kettle Pond Writers' Conference, the Key West Literary Seminar, and Martha's Vineyard Institute of Creative Writing. In spring and summer 2025, she will be an artist and writer in residence at the Writers' Colony at Dairy Hollow and Château d'Orquevaux. *I Might Trust You* is her first full-length short fiction collection.

Publication Credits

The Bitchin' Kitsch – "Macaw"
Bulb Culture Collective – "What if we were just two horses in a river"
Bullshit Lit: An Anthology – "Fishers Affair"
Bullshit Lit Chapbook – "Keeping track of February"
Club Plum – "Mint Winter Egg"
Cutbow Quarterly – "This isn't another story of how we counted money in Hell, but it could be"
The Disappointed Housewife – "Sugar Tide"
Dogwood Alchemy – "During which I make up a series of lies for you in August"
Eunoia Review – "Instructions for Dinner," "When we break up I am no longer a mermaid," "Coward," "Sublime," "We are connected," and "I try not to wonder about you"
Feral Mag – "Manhattan in January / and my heart was the evening"
Four Palaces – "Prism"
Giving Room Mag – "I keep following you home / maybe this time we'll be beautiful"
Gone Lawn – "I have a crush on a bog" and "That summer, my heart was an apple"
Harbor Review – "I can't find you by the shore anymore but I pretend you're still here / we make

dinner for our children"
Harpy Hybrid Review "W." and "Say"
JAKE The Anti-Literature Magazine – "When the woman you have a crush on asks you to host a séance, you say yes"
Litmora Lit Mag – "Pycnogonid"
Live Nude Poems – "Night Tide"
The Lumiere Review – "Goldfield"
The Massachusetts Poetry Festival First Poem Contest – "Back When the Deer Were Horses and the Horses Were Rivers"
The Missouri Review – "Sirens are mermaids with knives" and "Coward"
Moot Point Mag – "During which the witches descend into the haunted house together"
The Nassau Review – "Soft Livestock Threat" and "Mother"
New Lyricist, Issue 1 – "Cherry"
Orangepeel mag – "Red/Restaurant/Cherry/Father," "Summer Life" and "Dicentra"
Poetica Review – "What to do" and "I am running out of ways to say"
Prose Poems – "Tell me you want to know and we'll go from there"
Quailbell Mag – "Once more into the nicotine"
Querencia Press – "Melt"
Rogue Agent – "The softer the orange, the tastier the gold"

Rough Cut Press – "Nobody"
South Florida Poetry Journal – "The Saint"
Suburban Witchcraft – "I will be wonderful tomor
row," "Mythology is nothing like the truth," and
"You could have stitched a goodbye into the lining
of a pastry/
 I'd still want more"
the tide rises, the tide falls – "Corallium"
Trampset Review – "Oignon Brûlé"

Further EIF Titles

The Colourblind Grief
by Jude Gorini
ISBN: 9781739404406

A rip-roaring ride of a confessional novel, which takes place within the gay club scene of East London, before moving to Europe and the serene, sandy beaches of La Graciosa. Jude Gorini has written a brave, uncompromising tale which deals with issues of mental health, sexual identity and self-discovery. Difficult to put down, and impossible to forget!

Inner Passage
by Marlene Lee
ISBN: 9781739404468

This collection introduces the reader to an array of characters from the Midwest, Pacific Northwest, California, and the South whose lives lead them toward truths they ignore, resist, and explore — sometimes all at the same time.

To Catch a Poem
by Ingrid Wilson
ISBN: 9781739404475

From Bannerdale to Bewcastle, Cullercoats to Cald-
beck, poet Ingrid Wilson criss-crosses the Northern
countryside, searching for lines of poetry hidden in
high places and wooded hollows. Nature is her place
of worship, and poetry her song of praise.

Archery in the UK
by Nick Reeves and Ingrid Wilson
ISBN: 9781739757786

Inspired by the *Lyrical Ballads* of Wordsworth and
Coleridge, two authors set out to pen a contempo-
rary homage to this timeless collection. As the col-
laboration progresses, however, the poetry and the
unique narrative it carries takes on a life of its own.

Wounds I Healed
Edited by Gabriela Marie Milton
ISBN: 9781739757724
Award-winning authors, Pushcart nominees, voices
of women and men, come to the fore in this stunning, powerful, and unique anthology. These poems
testify both to the challenges that women face in
our society, and to their power to overcome them.

In The Shadow of Rainbows
by Selma Martin
ISBN: 9781739404444

In this dazzling debut poetry collection of over 60 carefully selected poems, author Selma Martin points the way to the beauty in the everyday, the shadow of the rainbow, and the silver lining at the edge of every cloud.

Three-Penny Memories
by Barbara Harris Leonhard
ISBN: 9781739757762

"Do you love your mother?"
This provocative question provides the catalyst for this stunning poetic memoir from Barbara Harris Leonhard. Through her artfully-crafted poetry, the author considers where her love and loyalties lie following her aging mother's diagnosis with Alzheimer's.

Re-Create and Celebrate
by Cindy Georgakas
ISBN: 9781739404413
In this unique book, Cindy guides her readers through simple steps to achieve the life they have always dreamed of.

9 781739 404499